Emily Harvale lives in Ea~~~~~~~
although she would prefe~~~~~~
Alps…or Canada…or anywhere that has several
months of snow. Emily loves snow almost as much
as she loves Christmas.

Having worked in the City (London) for several
years, Emily returned to her home town of
Hastings where she spends her days writing. And
wondering if it will snow.

You can contact her via her website, Twitter,
Facebook or Instagram.

There is also a Facebook group where fans can
chat with Emily about her books, her writing day
and life in general. Details are on the 'For You'
page of Emily's website.

Author contacts:
www.emilyharvale.com
www.twitter.com/emilyharvale
www.facebook.com/emilyharvalewriter
www.instagram.com/emilyharvale

***

Scan the code above to see all Emily's books on Amazon

Also by this author

Highland Fling
Lizzie Marshall's Wedding
The Golf Widows' Club
Sailing Solo
Carole Singer's Christmas
Christmas Wishes
A Slippery Slope
The Perfect Christmas Plan
Be Mine
It Takes Two
Bells and Bows on Mistletoe Row

The Goldebury Bay series:
Ninety Days of Summer – book 1
Ninety Steps to Summerhill – book 2
Ninety Days to Christmas – book 3

The Hideaway Down series:
A Christmas Hideaway – book 1
Catch A Falling Star – book 2
Walking on Sunshine – book 3
Dancing in the Rain – book 4

Hall's Cross series
Deck the Halls – book 1
The Starlight Ball – book 2

Michaelmas Bay series
Christmas Secrets in Snowflake Cove – book 1
Blame it on the Moonlight – book 2

Lily Pond Lane series
The Cottage on Lily Pond Lane –
Part One – New beginnings and Summer secrets
Part Two – Autumn leaves and Trick or treat
Christmas on Lily Pond Lane
Return to Lily Pond Lane
A Wedding on Lily Pond Lane

A

Wedding

on

Lily Pond Lane

Emily Harvale

Copyright © 2019 by Emily Harvale.

Emily Harvale has asserted her right to be identified as the author of this work.

No part of this publication may be reproduced, stored in a retrieval system, or transmitted, in any form or by any means, electronic, mechanical, photocopying, recording or otherwise, without the prior written permission of the publisher.

This book is a work of fiction. Names, characters, organisations, businesses, places and events other than those clearly in the public domain, are either the product of the author's imagination or are used fictitiously. Any resemblance to actual persons, living or dead, events or locales is entirely coincidental.

ISBN 978-1-909917-42-2

Published by Crescent Gate Publishing

Print edition published worldwide 2019
E-edition published worldwide 2019

Editor Christina Harkness

Cover design by JR and Emily Harvale

To Rachel Gilbey and all the fabulous
Bookbloggers who have shared the love of my
Lily Pond Lane series with their wonderful
reviews and support.
Thank you so much for helping to make
this series, sparkle.
You're stars! Each and every one of you.

Acknowledgements

My grateful thanks go to the following:

Christina Harkness for her patience and care in editing this book.
My webmaster, David Cleworth who does so much more than website stuff.
My cover design team, JR.
Luke Brabants. Luke is a talented artist and can be found at: www.lukebrabants.com
My wonderful friends for their friendship and love. You know I love you all.
All the fabulous members of my Readers' Club. You help and support me in so many ways and I am truly grateful for your ongoing friendship. I wouldn't be where I am today without you.
My Twitter and Facebook friends, and fans of my Facebook author page. It's great to chat with you. You help to keep me (relatively) sane!
Thank you for buying this book.

A Wedding on Lily Pond Lane

Chapter One

'That's it then?' Mia glanced at Jet who was sitting beside her at the kitchen table in Little Pond Farm, also staring at the laptop screen and the email Mia had just received from Glen Fox, the vicar of St Michael and All Angels.

Jet's eyes twinkled and his mouth broke into a beaming smile. He nodded and wrapped an arm around Mia's shoulder, gently squeezing the bare skin at the base of her neck with his fingers.

'That's it, my darling fiancée. Saturday May the 25th. The day you become Mrs Mia Cross.' The smile faltered momentarily. 'Or do you want to be Mrs Mia Ward-Cross?'

Mia grinned and coquettishly tossed a lock of golden brown hair from her face. 'I quite like the idea of you becoming Mr Jet Ward. What would you think about that? In this day and age why should the woman take the man's name, and not the other way around?'

Jet laughed, leant forward and kissed the tip of her nose. 'That's fine with me. As long as you're my wife and I'm your husband I don't care what we're called.'

Mia kissed him on the cheek. He meant it. He wouldn't care. Jet wasn't one of those men who needed people to think he was the dominant partner – the bread-winner, or whatever. He didn't mind that everyone in Little Pondale knew Mia had more money than him. He didn't care that everyone said that he was a changed man because of Mia. He didn't even mind that yesterday, and for the next few days, no doubt, everyone in the village would be talking about what happened between him and Alexia in The Frog and Lily the day before, and the fact that it had taken a kiss from Alexia to make him see sense about that nonsense with Mia and Garrick. Jet was his own man. All that mattered to him was that he loved Mia and she loved him. And that their relationship was securely back on track – especially now that they had the confirmation email from Glen about the date they'd picked for their wedding.

In spite of her tongue-in-cheek suggestion, Mia wanted to be Mrs Cross. She wanted that more than she had ever wanted anything in her life. She wanted to be his. Okay it was old- fashioned, but she didn't care. She wanted the world to know that Jet Cross, the man nobody ever thought would embark on a long-term relationship let alone get married, had chosen her to spend his life with; to grow old with. Every day she would wake up and thank her lucky stars for her good fortune. And for great-aunt Mattie, of course, without whom, none of this would be possible.

It did irritate Mia that Jet still wouldn't see her inheritance as shared funds though, but perhaps that would finally change once they were married. After all, she didn't think of Little Pond Farm as partly hers; it was Jet's farm and he'd worked hard to get it. But after their wedding, she would definitely see it as her forever-home.

'I want to be Mrs Cross.' She looked deep into his eyes and loved what she saw there. 'And I want to make a list of what needs to be done, asap, so sex will have to wait.'

He arched his brows in mock indignation. 'Who said anything about sex?'

She grinned at him. 'Your eyes did. I've told you before, I can tell what you're thinking just by looking at those gorgeous eyes of yours.'

He shut them tight. 'Can you tell what I'm thinking now?'

She laughed. 'Still about sex. It's all you ever think about.'

He opened one eye. 'You can talk. But that's not quite true. All I ever think about is you. Sex is merely the icing on that particular cake.'

'Ooh! Cake. I love you, Jet.'

Jet opened the other eye and leant forward again as Mia typed the words, wedding cake, into the internet browser and images of several grand confections filled the laptop screen. 'I love you too. Er. We're not going to have some massive creation that looks more like the Taj Mahal than an iced sponge cake, are we?'

'No. I'd rather have something simple but pretty. A bit like Ella.' She turned to Jet and giggled. 'Don't tell her I said that.'

'She'd be the first to say something like that herself. And she knows you think she's brilliant.' He kissed the top of Mia's head as he stood up. 'Well, if we're not having sex, I may as well go and run the farm. Unless there's anything you need me to do right now in respect of the wedding preparations?'

Mia shook her head. 'Not at the moment, thanks. I'll give you a list when I've sorted some of it out. I'm going to ask Jenny to make the cake, I think. Provided she's happy to. Is that okay with you?'

'Absolutely. I love Jenny's cakes.'

'And what about having the reception at The Frog and Lily?'

'The pub? Are you sure?' His voice held a hint of concern. 'Don't get me wrong. I couldn't be happier than to walk across the road from the church to the pub, but is that really what you want? Money's no object, is it? You can book one of the Grand Hotels nearby if you like. You can have your dream wedding. I know we don't have much time to organise it, but I'd hate you to make do with something if it isn't exactly what you want. You're only going to get married once, Mia.

Believe me. I'm not letting you get away ever again.'

Mia smiled at him. 'The only thing I want is to marry you. Yes, a posh hotel would be lovely, but they have to be booked months in advance. I don't want to delay our wedding just so that the reception can be a big affair. I don't think I even want a big affair. Hettie and Fred's wedding was wonderful, wasn't it? Apart from you and me nearly being killed when Tom pushed that stone angel statue from its corbel, of course. They had their reception in the pub and everyone had a fabulous time.'

He nodded. 'That's true. But think about it first. Talk to your mum. And to Ella. I'm sure they'll both have some suggestions.' He bent down and kissed her on the lips. 'Right. I'm off. Yell if you need me.'

She glanced up as he neared the door leading out to the farmyard. 'How do you feel about pink and white? And possibly a bit of blue?'

'For the cake? Or to decorate the pub?' Little M jumped out of her bed beside the Range and scampered across the tiled, kitchen floor towards Jet as he placed a hand on the doorknob.

'For the theme. Bridesmaids, invitations, flowers, cake, decorations. The whole shebang.'

He looked thoughtful for a second and Little M looked up at him as if she were giving the matter equal consideration – when in reality, the dog was probably wondering why her master wasn't opening the door for them both to go outside.

'Sounds good to me. Providing I don't have to wear a white suit, a pink shirt and a blue top hat.' He winked at her, blew her a kiss and almost tripped over Little M as the dog dashed out in front of him the moment he opened the door. Shaking his head, he smiled at Mia. 'Assuming this little rascal doesn't kill me beforehand.' He closed the door and left Mia to it.

She jumped up, grabbed the landline phone and called Ella at Sunbeam Cottage, completely forgetting that it was still only seven-thirty in the morning and not everyone would have been up for more than two hours. Garrick answered.

'Oh. Er. Hi, Garrick. Is Ella there?'

'Hi, Mia. She's still in bed. Is everything okay? I ... I heard that you and Jet have ... sorted things out. I also heard what Alexia did in the pub. I'm really sorry I caused such a mess, but I'm glad you're back together. You are back together, aren't you?'

'Yes, we are. We definitely are.'

A soft sigh wafted down the phone. 'That's a relief. I would never have forgiven myself if you were miserable because of me.'

'It's fine, Garrick. Let's forget it. That's what Jet and I have decided to do. We talked it through yesterday and last night and we're not even going to mention it again.'

The less said about Garrick's kiss and that it could possibly have had the potential to end Mia and Jet's relationship, the better as far as Mia was concerned. Although Jet had told her during their 'make up sex' that even if she had actually kissed Garrick, he probably would've forgiven her. Eventually. He couldn't bear the thought of not having her in his life now.

'Oh. Okay. Um. Can I give Ella a message? Or shall I just ask her to call you back?'

'Get her to call me, please. As soon as she gets up. It's important.'

'Right you are.'

'Garrick.' Mia heard Flora's gurgles. The baby was no doubt in Garrick's arms, probably having her feed. 'How's Flora?' That wasn't what she was going to say, but it gave her time to think.

'As gorgeous as ever. She slept a little later this morning so I'm trying to feed her now.'

'Sorry. I'll let you go then.'

'Mia?'

'Yes.'

'Was there something else you were going to say?'

Mia sucked in a breath. Garrick knew her so well.

'Yes. But I'm not sure I should tell you over the phone.'

'You've set the date, haven't you? For your wedding.'

How did he know that? She'd only just seen the email from Glen this morning confirming it. Although they had said yesterday that they wanted whatever date Glen had in May. Perhaps someone had overheard that. Or maybe Glen had mentioned it to Jenny and Jenny had ... oh what did it matter how he knew.

'Yes. It's May the 25th.'

Garrick made an odd sound. 'Will I be invited? Or should I keep my distance?'

'You'll be invited, Garrick. But I would think twice about going to rugby practice this week, just in case.' She gave a little laugh. 'That was a joke. I think. Or maybe not.'

'I'd rather face him and get it over with. I wouldn't blame Jet for punching me, quite frankly, but I feel I should apologise to his face. I hope we can still be friends ... in time.'

'I don't think he'll bear a grudge. It's water under the bridge, and thanks to Alexia, he doesn't feel betrayed or anything. Now that he understands exactly what happened and why. At least not by me. And he knows you're ... well, that you're grieving. I don't think he blames you either, really. But he'll probably tell you not to do it again. Ever.'

'It'll never happen again. I can promise you that.'

'Okay. That's that then. Get Ella to call me, right?'

'The minute she stumbles down the stairs and demands coffee, I'll let her know you called. Bye, Mia.'

Mia hung up and leant against the worktop. How would Jet react when he saw Garrick? Yesterday, when they talked it through, Jet said he would forgive him. That he would let it go. And it certainly seemed to be forgotten between Jet and Mia. They'd made love a number of times during the day yesterday, when they got back from Corner Cottage, and again last night. And since agreeing not to mention it, neither of them had spoken of either Garrick's kiss, or Alexia's. It was a hiccup. And it was forgotten. But was it? Was it really?

The ringing phone made Mia jump. But the caller display showed her mum's name, not Ella's.

'So?' Lori asked the second Mia answered. 'Is it the 25th, or not?'

Mia had found time to call her mum yesterday and tell her that not only had she and Jet made up, but that they'd asked Glen to set the date, and they were just waiting for his confirmation before announcing it to everyone.

Mia laughed excitedly. 'Yep. It's the 25th. I want to go to London as soon as possible. I need to find a dress, and get the bridesmaids' dresses and … well, everything. I'm waiting for Ella to call me back and then I was going to call you. I know you said you were free today, but I think Ella said she may be busy and I want the three of us to go together.'

'Today? You want to go to London today?'

'Well, yes. I don't have much time, Mum. The wedding's in a little over three months and I haven't a clue where to start.'

'The invitations are the first thing you need to sort out, sweetheart. That's the May Bank Holiday weekend, I think, and people will soon start making plans. The sooner you send the invites out, the better. Have you made a list?'

'I've just started. I've got the cake, the reception venue, the–'

'I meant a guest list, darling. Of who you want to invite. And who Jet will want. You need to get that down on paper asap. Give me half an hour. I'll come round for coffee and we can make a start.'

Without waiting for a reply, Lori rang off.

A guest list? Of course that should be the first thing to do. But she'd need to get Jet to help with that. Other than the villagers, his half-sister Tiffany and her fiancé, Mia had no idea who Jet might want at his wedding. She wasn't even sure who she wanted to invite. This was going to be more difficult than she had thought.

Chapter Two

Breanna Wright started at one end of the rack and slowly worked her way along, quietly oohing and ahhing over each exquisite dress wrapped in its protective polythene cover. She took her time to admire every detail as if she were standing in one of the viewing rooms in The National Gallery studying works of art, not loitering in a bridal shop in London's West End, drooling over wedding dresses. In her opinion, these dresses were works of art. Some of them had price tags to match. One dress Breanna particularly liked was priced at fifteen thousand pounds. Fifteen. Thousand. Pounds! Admittedly, that was a snip compared to what some brides were prepared to pay but fifteen thousand pounds was enough to make most potential bride's eyes water.

Not that Breanna was a potential bride. But not for the want of wishing. She had dreamt of being a bride since she was six, and had her first crush on a friend's twin brother, but at thirty-four, and once again, boyfriend-less, the prospect seemed even more remote than it had back then. The day she declared her feelings to the six-year-old boy of her dreams and foolishly tried to kiss him on the cheek. He'd turned at the last minute and she'd planted a wet sloppy smacker right on his lips. He had been horrified. He'd made a big thing of wiping his mouth with his sleeve ... several times; sticking his tongue out as if he wanted to be sick and finally running away, shouting that he only liked girls with red hair, not girls with hair the colour of soot. He had apologised later; his sister had made him, but Breanna knew then that she would never stand a chance of getting him to ask her to be his girlfriend, let alone make her his bride.

A few years later, Breanna wasn't simply dreaming of being a bride. She was dreaming of being a wedding planner too. A world-famous wedding planner, no less. With a penthouse apartment overlooking the Thames, where super-star clients who had begged to be on her list, would come for cocktails, if they were lucky enough to be invited to her inner sanctum. Those who weren't would go to one of her offices in London, Paris or New York. *The Wright Wedding* being the go-to business for anyone who was anyone, and in need of the perfect, dream wedding.

But that was all it was – a dream. And probably always would be, despite her telling everyone throughout her years at school, that she would be a wedding-planner. What would they think if they could see her now? If they knew she worked in Sainsbury's. On the check-outs. Not that there was anything wrong with that. But it was a far cry from what she had dreamt of doing. Would they laugh at her? Would they feel sorry for her? Would they tell her there was still time for her to pursue her dreams? That was what she told herself. And had done for more years than she could remember.

Her salary from Sainsbury's was good, all things considered, and she lived at home with her mum, but after paying her share of bills and general living expenses, she never managed to save enough money to get her dream business off the ground.

Things would only get worse in the months to come. Her mum was selling their house and moving to a brand new, one-bedroom apartment in a local retirement village. She had discussed it fully with Breanna before making her decision and although it meant Breanna would have to find somewhere else to live, it was what Madeleine Wright wanted, and with deteriorating health, Green Oaks Village in a leafy suburb of Bromley, was the best place for her.

Breanna had been offered a room in a friend's house, and whilst the rent was more than she paid her mum, with few other options, Breanna had agreed to take it. The day she said yes, was the day she realised, once and for all, *The Wright Wedding* was never going to happen. Not unless some miracle occurred. And in Breanna's life to date, those had been in very short supply. Non-existent, in fact.

This outing to the bridal shop was meant to cheer her up. A final hurrah to her dreams, and an unwelcome hello to her new reality.

'Does madam require assistance?'

The eagle-eyed sales girl had been watching Breanna since the moment she stepped into the shop. Breanna had told her twice already that she was 'merely browsing'.

Breanna threw her a brief smile. 'No thank you. Still browsing.'

Eagle-eye swooped closer. 'Perhaps if madam would provide me with an idea of what it is madam wants, I may be able to find exactly what madam seeks.'

Was she for real?

'I'm not sure what it is I want, exactly, but I'm certain I'll know when I see it, thank you.'

Breanna had no doubt the woman would have persisted, but the somewhat tinny rendition of the most well-known section of the *Bridal Chorus* announced that someone else had entered the shop and Eagle-eye flew away, probably hoping that this new customer would be more amenable.

'Thanks. But we'd like to have a look around if that's okay,' the customer said in reply to Eagle-eye's offer of assistance.

Something about the voice seemed familiar but Breanna didn't want to turn around in case

Eagle-eye misread the situation as a request for help. Besides, Breanna had just found the dress of her dreams.

'Oh hello, Gorgeous,' she whispered to herself, removing the flowing gown from the rail and slipping one arm behind it to sweep it up in order to get a better look at it. Ivory silk with a pearl encrusted bodice and hand-embroidered lace sleeves, it was elegant and simple and yet stunning and detailed at the same time. Breanna couldn't resist taking a peek beneath the polythene and delicately brushing her fingers against the cultured pearls.

'Breanna? Is that you?'

'Mia? Mia Ward?' Breanna felt like a schoolgirl again as she spun round to face her childhood friend. But as she did so, the clasp of her bracelet caught on a row of pearls and the dress crumpled towards the floor as one by one, each delicate pearl came loose from the fine stitching holding it in place and plopped onto the floor, tumbling in the direction of Eagle-eye and her horror-stricken face.

Breanna was mortified. Not simply because she had possibly ruined an exceedingly expensive dress, but also because Mia Ward was not alone. Her mum, Lori was with her, but more importantly, so was Ella Swann.

This was so humiliating. All three of them would obviously assume that she was engaged. Why else would a woman be looking at wedding dresses? Because she was a saddo and this was her only dream in life? There was no way she was admitting to that. But Lori Ward and Breanna's mum still sent each other Christmas cards. They were possibly even friends on Facebook. Breanna couldn't say she was engaged in case it got back to her mum. Madeleine Wright would quickly extinguish that flicker of hope.

Breanna could say she was looking at dresses for a friend. No. No one would believe that. But they might believe she was looking for a dress for a client. A client of her wedding-planning business, *The Wright Wedding*.

That's what she would tell them if they asked. There was a slight chance they wouldn't. But if they did, she could possibly get her mum to back her up on that, couldn't she? Her mum knew being a wedding planner had been Breanna's life-long dream. She could tell her mum that she had finally decided to take the plunge and start it. After all, one little white lie never did any harm, did it?

But now wasn't the time to worry about lying. Eagle-eye was virtually prostrate on the floor, trying to retrieve a few of the pearls that had rolled beneath a large and heavy-looking shelf unit, on which various tiaras sparkled in the bright, shop lights, and etched champagne flutes glistened amongst floral clips and diamante necklaces, earrings and bracelets.

'Perhaps I can reach them,' Breanna offered, smiling wanly at Mia, Lori and Ella as she freed her bracelet from the dress and hastily placed the damaged garment back on the rack before getting onto her knees beside Eagle-eye. 'My arms are longer than yours.'

'I think you've done quite enough already, madam,' came the curt reply.

'I didn't do it on purpose. And I'm truly sorry. Please. Let me help.'

'Yeah,' said Ella. 'Let her.'

Reluctantly, Eagle-eye withdrew her arm and shifted over a few centimetres whilst Mia, Lori and Ella exchanged glances and gave Breanna reassuring smiles.

Breanna's limbs were definitely longer and her fingers immediately felt the smooth, silk-like surface of the runaway pearls. Clasping them tightly, she pulled her arm back quickly so as not to let them go, but as she did so, her elbow hit Eagle-eye in, well, one of her eyes. The poor girl shrieked, leapt to her feet, stumbled over Breanna's leg as Breanna attempted to stand, and finally careered into the shelving, sending jewels, glasses and all and sundry, flying into the air.

Breanna rapidly stepped out of harm's way. 'Technically, that wasn't entirely my fault.'

Eagle-eye's language turned decidedly blue.

'I'll sort it out,' Mia said, nodding at Lori and Ella, who hurriedly ushered Breanna away before Eagle-eye could murder her.

The *Bridal Chorus* rang out when Ella yanked open the shop door.

'Ooh!' said Ella, clearly trying hard not to laugh. 'I've just realised what that's meant to be. It's *Here Comes the Bride*, isn't it? That's a bit tacky for such a posh-looking shop.'

Lori tutted and shoved Ella out. 'The shop's not quite so posh-looking now. I hope the place is insured.'

'I don't know what happened,' Breanna said, gulping and trying to stop her legs from shaking. 'That dress looked ultra-expensive.'

Lori nodded. 'It did. But Mia will calm the assistant down. I'm sure it'll all be fine.'

'I wouldn't bank on that,' said Ella, linking her arm through Breanna's, just like the old days when they were friends at school. 'But if it's not, Mia will work something out. She's good like that.'

The three of them stood outside for a moment or two, looking in on the devastation as Mia obviously attempted to placate Eagle-eye, who now had one eye turning a delightful shade of purple, to match the vivid colour of both her cheeks and her ever-increasingly foul language. They could hear the expletives even with the door closed.

'I think we should move away from the window,' Lori added, when Eagle-eye glowered at Breanna and looked as if she might throw something.

'Well, Bree,' Ella said, giving Breanna a friendly nudge. 'You've just given *Bridezilla* a whole new meaning.'

Chapter Three

'Wow!' Breanna said, clutching the stem of her wine glass with a shaking hand several minutes later. When Mia had exited the shop, told Breanna not to worry about a thing, and suggested the three of them pop into the pub a few doors away while Mia stayed and sorted everything out, Breanna had been more than grateful. Now, she was amazed. Mia had told her about great-aunt Matilda Ward and the inheritance she had left Mia. 'So you're rich?'

Mia nodded and smiled. 'Exceedingly. And as I said, there's no need for you to worry about a thing. Diana, the sales assistant, spoke to the owners and they agreed that accidents happen. They're prepared to forget the whole thing, but I think you should look elsewhere for your wedding dress. Oh, and congratulations, by the way.'

'What? Oh, I'm not engaged.'

'You're not?' Mia looked confused and glanced at Breanna's ring-less hand.

'Why were you looking at wedding dresses then?' Ella asked.

'Oh. Er. For a client.' And there it was. The little white lie.

'A client?' Lori queried.

'Of my wedding-planning business, *The Wright Wedding*.' And there was the second white lie.

'You did it?' Mia sounded impressed. 'Bree, that's fantastic news.'

Lori glanced over the rim of her wine glass. 'I don't recall Madeleine mentioning you'd got a business, in her Christmas cards.'

'Er. Didn't she?' Breanna slipped a finger between the neck of her sweater and her increasingly flushed skin and tried to give herself some air. 'She probably didn't want to jinx it. You know what my mum's like. Superstitious about everything. Neither of us was sure it would be a success. She obviously decided to keep quiet about it.' Well, this lying was easy. A bit too easy, in fact. Breanna was almost enjoying herself. She turned her attention back to Mia. 'But are you sure everything's okay at the shop? You … you didn't have to pay her, or the owners, did you? If you did, I'd rather you told me. None of it was your fault.'

Mia reached out and squeezed Breanna's arm. 'It was partly my fault. I made you jump when I said your name. You were in a world of your own. I could see that from your face. If I hadn't startled you, you wouldn't have caught your bracelet on the dress. Everything else that happened was as a consequence of that, so you see, it was my fault. But if it puts your mind at ease, I only gave Diana a hundred pounds, which is nothing, believe me. And I promised the owners that I'd pay for the repairs to the dress and any damage caused if they can't claim it all on their insurance.'

'Oh my God! That could cost a fortune.' Breanna was sure she was going to be sick and clamped a hand across her mouth, staring at Mia with terror-filled eyes. One hundred pounds might not be much to Mia now, but to Breanna, that sum was almost equivalent to her monthly grocery bill. 'I … I don't have that sort of money.'

Mia smiled. 'But I do. Honestly, Bree. Don't worry about it. It's all sorted.'

'But I'll never be able to pay you back.'

'Pay me back?' Mia frowned and shook her head. 'You don't need to pay me back. I told you. It was my fault I made you jump. Now let's change the subject.'

Breanna tutted. 'That's ridiculous, Mia. I really appreciate it but…' She let her voice trail off. What was she thinking? She couldn't offer to pay. It would take her a lifetime. And Mia had just told her that she was loaded. She gave Mia a grateful smile. 'Well, if you're really sure then thank you. Thank you so much. Money is a bit tight at the moment so you've actually saved my life. What with mum selling the house, and me having to move. Well, my salary at Sainsbury's is pretty much spoken for.'

'Sainsbury's?' Ella asked. 'I thought you had your own business?'

'What? Oh yes. I do. Er. But it's still early days and starting a business costs an absolute fortune. Who knew?' Breanna laughed but even to her ears, it sounded fake. 'I work part-time as a cashier to help things along. Just until the business really takes off, you know? Anyway, Mia. Thanks again. And thanks for the drink, but I really should get going.' She tried to stand but her legs were shaking and she pressed the tips of her fingers on the table top for balance. 'Er. It was lovely seeing you all again after so many years. And if there's ever anything I can do to repay you, Mia, you know where I am.' She forced a smile and was about to walk away when Ella's next words stopped her.

'Not if you're moving, we won't. Know where you are, I mean. You should give us your number so that we can keep in touch. And what's the rush, anyway? It's almost lunchtime. Why don't you join us and fill us in on what's been happening to you over all these years? And tell us a bit more about your business.'

'Yes!' Mia looked suddenly excited. Animated even. 'And there is something you can do for me, Bree. Well, something we can do for each other. I'm getting married. And you're a wedding planner. This must be Fate! We were meant to bump into each other in that shop. Oh Bree! I think it's you who may be saving my life. I thought wedding planning would be fun. But it isn't. It really isn't. I only started this morning and by the time we got on the train to come here, my head was splitting. Everyone I met in the village this morning had suggestions and ideas. Honestly. I don't know where to start. Say you'll do it, Bree. Please, please say you'll be my wedding planner.'

'That's an excellent idea,' Lori piped up.

'Yes,' Ella said, looking slightly less enthusiastic than Mia and her mum, and a little more sceptical. 'It's almost too good to be true.'

Chapter Four

Mia was over the moon. It had been the perfect shopping trip to London. Well, almost. Okay, she had had to pay for some of the damage to a bridal display and for an expensive dress to be repaired, but she'd found herself a wedding planner, and been reunited with an old schoolfriend she'd lost touch with, so it was worth every penny. And Jet would be pleased. He had tried to sound enthusiastic about the wedding preparations, but Mia knew it wasn't really his thing. Tell him to do something and he'd be fine. Ask him for suggestions, and not so much.

It had been the same at Christmas. Mia had planned all the decorations, the meals, the presents, even the sleigh and the reindeers, but Jet had put it all into action. Although that wasn't totally fair. He had planned the proposal and that was the most magical thing Mia had ever seen.

The truth was, all Jet wanted was to get married. He would've been happy going to the local registry office. It was Mia who wanted all 'the fluff and fizz' as Jet had called it at first – although he had quickly corrected himself and had since referred to it as 'the celebration'. He would definitely be relieved to know that someone else was taking over and that all that would be required of him was to do as he was told, and show up on the day. He would be a happy man. Even happier than he was this morning when Mia had left to catch the train to London.

'It was definitely Fate.' Mia rested the disposable coffee cup on the slightly icky-looking table as the rhythm of the train made the contents of her plastic-coated paper cup slosh to and fro, despite her steadying hand.

'It was definitely something,' Ella said, staring out of the window as city lights gave way to dark, country skies.

'What's up with you?' Mia leant across the table and slapped Ella's fingers. 'You've been acting weird ever since we left the pub.'

'No, I haven't.'

'Yes, you have,' Lori agreed.

Ella darted a look from Mia to Lori and back again, then sighed, leant forward and plopped her crossed arms on the table. 'Okay, perhaps I have. Doesn't this stuff with Bree and her business bother you even a little bit?'

Mia frowned. 'What happened in the shop was an accident. It was the sort of thing that would normally happen to you or me. And I did make her jump. It's only fair that I should pay. Why do you keep harping on about it?'

Ella arched her brows. 'I don't keep harping on about it.'

Lori tutted. 'Again, I have to agree with Mia. You brought it up at least three times this afternoon.'

Ella's mouth dropped open and she stared at them.

Mia smiled. 'You'll still get to have lots of input into the wedding. You're my best friend. The sister I never had. Not forgetting, you're also my maid of honour. There's no need to be jealous or anything.'

'Jealous?' Several heads turned in Ella's direction at her high-pitched shriek. She lowered her voice and leant further forward. 'I'm not jealous. Yes. I want to be involved. And yes, I want to do anything I can to help, but I'm definitely not jealous. I have absolutely no idea how to plan a wedding. The thing is, I'm not so sure that Bree does, either. That's all I'm saying. I mean, how do you know she's any good at planning a wedding? She admitted she works part-time in Sainsbury's, so she can't be making much money from her business. And how long has she had it? Didn't you notice that every time I asked her a question about it, she gave some ridiculous answer or changed the subject?'

Mia and Lori exchanged glances.

'That's true,' said Lori. 'And it is a little odd that Madeleine didn't mention it in her Christmas card. I know Bree said that was because her mum is superstitious and didn't want to jinx it, but that would indicate that Bree only started the business recently.'

'So?' Mia pursed her lips. 'Gill, Ella and I have only recently started writing our novel. It doesn't mean we won't be any good at it.'

Ella smirked. 'Actually, I think you and I have both realised that it'll be Gill who does most of the writing. We were supposed to start last year, and we used every excuse in the book not to, so that's probably not your best argument.'

Mia tutted. 'Okay. That wasn't a good example. But just because someone is trying something new, it doesn't follow that they won't be successful. And it's all Bree's ever wanted to do. Surely you remember her at school? She had all those notebooks crammed with her with drawings, and pictures she'd cut out of magazines. She'd even designed her business logo, remember? It was a love heart, with a ribbon wrapped around it, and the ends were held aloft by two white doves. Or was it butterflies? And maybe it was pale pink. Anyway, it had *The Wright Wedding* emblazoned across the ribbon ... in diamonds, I think. Well, glittery stickers to represent diamonds.'

Ella nodded. 'I do remember that. But that makes it even more weird. When I asked her for a business card what did she say?'

'Er.' Mia thought for a moment. 'That she was having a new batch reprinted because she had run out. What's weird about that? It shows lots of people want her card. Or at least that she's handing them out and trying to drum up business.'

Ella shook her head. 'Does it?'

'Oh I see,' said Lori, nodding. 'What you're saying is that the real reason she didn't have any cards is because she doesn't have any. That she doesn't have a business.'

'That's exactly what I'm saying.' Ella looked Mia in the eye. 'Didn't you notice how terrified she looked when you asked her to be your wedding planner? She looked as if she wanted to bolt. And she couldn't wait to get away. I mean, who in their right mind would turn down a free lunch, especially when that lunch came with a guaranteed opportunity to discuss possibly the biggest deal her supposed business is ever likely to have?'

'She said she had to get to Sainsbury's, and didn't want to be late for her shift,' Mia said, defensively. 'That's completely understandable.'

'Perhaps. But you still had to ask her twice for her telephone number and I'm pretty sure she did everything she could to try to avoid giving it to you. In fact, how do you know she gave you her number? She could've given you a fake one.'

'Why would she do that?' Mia pulled her phone from her handbag and scrolled through her contacts for Breanna's number.

Ella sighed and strung out her words. 'Because she hasn't got a business.'

'There's one way to find out,' Lori suggested. 'I could call Madeleine when I get home. I don't have her number on me because we only send Christmas cards to one another now, but I'm sure I've got it somewhere, and she hasn't moved yet.'

'Or I could simply call Bree and ask,' Mia said, tapping the number and holding the phone to her ear.

Ella pulled a face. 'And she could simply lie again.'

Mia pulled a face in return, but after a few moments said: 'It's gone to voicemail.' Then: 'Oh hi, Bree. It's Mia. We're on the train and by the time you get this message we might be back in Little Pondale, where, as I mentioned, there's no mobile reception. So call me on my home number, please. Um. I just need to discuss one or two things with you. About the wedding. And your business. And – Oh. It's cut me off.' She glanced at Ella and her mum.

'Did the voicemail mention *The Wright Wedding*? Or did it simply say Bree?' Ella flopped back against the seat, her arms still crossed in front of her.

Mia frowned. 'It simply said that my call could not be taken and I could leave a message after the tone. Which as you heard, is what I did.'

'Well,' said Lori, resting her head against the seatback. 'There's nothing we can do for now and it's been a very long day. You won't mind if I shut my eyes for five minutes, will you sweetheart?'

'Of course not, Mum. You go ahead. I'm going to flick through some of these bridal magazines to see if there's anything I like. I was a bit disappointed by the selection of dresses we saw today.'

Ella pulled another face. 'That's because you spent most of the day firstly sorting out Bree's little accident and secondly, trying to persuade her to be your wedding planner.' She held up her hands. 'Okay. That's a slight exaggeration. But we definitely didn't get to even half the shops you wanted to visit.'

Mia grinned at Ella. 'Which was actually because we all decided that going to the Christian Dior: Designer of Dreams Exhibition would be a worthwhile detour.'

'Which I believe it was,' said Lori, her eyes firmly closed but a huge smile on her lips. 'It's been such a long time since I last visited the V&A and some of those dresses were to die for.'

Ella smiled too, and let out a soft, dreamy sigh. 'Oh God, they were, weren't they? I'd love to be rich.' She sat bolt upright. 'That's it!'

Lori's eyes shot open. 'What's it?' she and Mia asked in unison.

'You're rich. You don't need to go to a shop to buy a dress. You can have one designed and handmade.'

Mia's eyes opened wide with excitement. 'I can! And the bridesmaids' dresses too if we can't find any we like. But can it be done in three months? We don't have much time.'

Ella grinned and settled back against the seat, her voice laced with sarcasm. 'Ask your wedding planner. If she's any good, she'll be able to get it done. And she'll have contacts, too. Assuming that she really is a wedding planner and not just working in Sainsbury's because as much as I love Sainsbury's I don't think they stock wedding dresses. Although I could be wrong.'

Mia tutted and tossed a couple of magazines at her. 'Oh, do shut up. Look through those and if you see any dresses you like, mark the pages. And not just bridesmaids' dresses for you, but also wedding dresses for me.'

'Hey! I'm not your wedding planner.' Ella sat up again and grabbed one of the magazines. 'Oh, okay. I'll shut up.'

Chapter Five

Breanna had never had much luck. What was the saying? If it wasn't for my bad luck, I'd have no luck at all. That certainly applied to Breanna. One of her exes had called her a walking disaster zone. Something always seemed to happen when Breanna was around. And not in a good way.

Take yesterday, for example. That could only happen to her. Anyone else would have easily removed their hand from the dress and turned to greet Mia, Lori and Ella calmly and cordially.

Anyone else would have said that they had just popped in on a whim to look at the dresses, and not been the slightest embarrassed. No one else would have lied to two old school friends, merely to save face. Hmm. That had certainly worked out well.

She listened to Mia's voice message for the umpteenth time and cringed yet again. Something in Mia's tone indicated she may be questioning Breanna's lie.

Breanna slumped against the seat on the top deck of the bus and stared out at the streets of London, wet and glistening from the sudden heavy downpour. She had been caught in it and was soaked to the skin.

When the rain started, she was clutching her takeaway coffee with one hand and had tried to open her umbrella with the other but a gust of wind had come from nowhere, caught her umbrella, turned it inside out and ripped it from her hand.

The last time she saw it, it was tumbling along Oxford Street after hitting an unsuspecting Japanese tourist in the face just as he was trying to take a photo of his female companion pointing at the Oxford Circus tube station sign.

As Breanna had run for her bus, thankfully still clutching her takeaway coffee with the lid firmly closed, she hoped the man's expensive-looking camera hadn't broken when he dropped it … and that it was waterproof, as he bent to retrieve it from the deep puddle in which it landed.

She did a quick double-take when the bus slowly trundled away from its stop. Was that her umbrella caught in the bare branches of that tree? It looked like a massive, multicoloured bloom and she couldn't help but smile.

Until a pungent smell assaulted her nose and a man, with hair so greasy that the rain had run off it straight onto his stained and filthy raincoat, plonked himself on the seat beside her in spite of the fact that there were several empty seats around.

'Terrible weather, eh love?' he said, grinning through the large gap in his teeth.

Breanna nodded and pressed herself against the window. 'Yes. Awful.'

'Long time since I've been on a bus.' His grin broadened. 'Must be my lucky day 'cos I found this on the floor in the bus shelter.' He held up a slightly damp, one day Travelcard and kissed it. 'No point in handing it in. It'll be out of date before I made it to lost property.' He gave her a friendly nudge with his elbow. 'Sometimes the gods smile on us, eh love?'

'Yes. Sometimes.' She forced a smile despite the fact that she was feeling a little nauseous.

And then she realised how lucky she was. This man was staring at the Travelcard as if he had won the lottery. Well, she *had* won the lottery. In a way. She had been given the chance to fulfil her lifelong ambition. She had been asked to plan Mia Ward's wedding. A wedding where it seemed, cost wasn't an issue.

As the bus sped down Regent Street, Breanna watched people dashing in and out of the famous shops, such as Liberty, and Hamleys and the flagship stores of several designer brands, and asked herself the question: Could she do it?

She had been dreaming of this opportunity all her life. How difficult could it actually be to plan someone's wedding? She had seen all the films, read all the books and was up-to-date with all the latest bridal magazines – another bonus from working in Sainsbury's. She knew what brides wanted on their wedding day. Surely it couldn't be too hard to find out how to get all that stuff, could it?

She was due some holiday. She could take a couple of weeks off work to plan Mia's wedding. It wouldn't take longer than that, would it? And she could take that Bank holiday weekend off, and the week before it, if she booked it now.

But could she really pull it off? Could she assuage any doubts Mia already had? Could she transform herself from a walking disaster zone to a professional and highly competent wedding planner?

In reality, probably not. And did she really want to continue lying to her old school friend? Especially as Mia had been so lovely to her yesterday. And so generous. Who knows what would have happened if Mia hadn't stepped in and sorted things out in that bridal shop. They might have called the police. They might have sued Breanna for the damage. Breanna closed her eyes and bit her lower lip, suddenly riddled with guilt and doubt. She let out a heavy sigh.

'You okay, love?' the man beside her asked.

She had forgotten he was there.

'What?' She nodded. 'Oh, yes, thank you.' Then she turned to face him. 'But I've told someone a lie and I feel really bad about it.'

The man shook his head. 'Was it a lie that would hurt them, or one that would make them feel better?'

'One that made me feel better. Except it doesn't now. I told a friend I could do something.'

'And you can't?'

Breanna shrugged. 'I might be able to. But not quite in the way that I said.'

He nodded and smiled wanly, a sage expression on his wizened face, but he didn't reply until a minute or two later as the bus raced past Piccadilly Circus and the flashing lights of the advertising hoardings.

'It's never good to lie to a friend. I lied to a friend. My best friend. My wife. And I've ended up like this, on a bus in the rain using someone else's Travelcard. Tell the truth, love. That's my advice. If the person is a friend, they'll understand, and they'll probably forgive you. Continue lying, and they'll be doubly hurt when they find out. Trust me. I know.'

She looked at him properly for the first time since he'd sat beside her. What was his story? He'd been married. Had he cheated? Was that his lie? Or was it drinking, or drugs, or gambling? Or something else? Clearly he had no intention of elaborating and he now stared straight ahead as the bus turned into Haymarket.

'You're right.' She nodded as if her head were on a spring and couldn't stop. 'You're absolutely right. My friend is lovely. And really kind-hearted.

I'm sure she'll forgive me. She may even give me a chance. And if she doesn't, I'm no worse off, really. I may lose the opportunity of a lifetime, but at least I won't be lying to a friend.' An idea popped into her head and she smiled. 'Excuse me please. I need to get off. We'll be nearing Charing Cross soon.'

He gave her an odd look but smiled back as he stood up. 'Going home? Or going to tell your friend you lied?'

She nodded. 'Going to see my friend. And to ask her if she'll give me a chance. She can only say no, right?'

'Right. Good luck, love. May the gods smile on you.'

Breanna thanked him and made her way towards the stairs. She turned, dashed back and handed the man her still-closed cup of coffee. 'Thank you. I haven't touched this if you'd like it. I'm not in the mood for coffee right now.'

'You sure?'

'Yes. And you'd be doing me a favour. I won't have to search for a bin. Sorry. That didn't come out right.'

He chuckled. 'I know what you meant, love. Thanks. It really is my lucky day. I hope it's just as lucky for you.'

'I hope so too. Have a lovely day.'

She smiled, pressed the bell on the post to let the driver know she wanted to get off and ran down the stairs. She jumped off at the stop and hurried across the road to the station where she bought a ticket, found the train was waiting, got on, got a seat and snuggled against the window, all without so much as even one tiny thing going wrong.

Perhaps things would work out, after all.

And then she remembered.

The reason she had gone to Oxford Street was to buy a present for a guy at work. It hadn't been expensive, just a jokey T-shirt from his favourite shop, but she had put it in one of the Sainsbury's carrier bags that she always had in her handbag, and she'd stuffed the plastic carrier bag beside her on the seat. And that was where she had left it.

She grinned to herself. The man who had sat next to her on the bus had said the gods were smiling on him today. She hoped he'd spot the T-shirt. And she prayed he wouldn't hand it in as lost property. A T-shirt worth ten quid would probably make his day.

Chapter Six

Breanna should have thought this through, but as she watched the train pull away, leaving her standing on the platform of a seemingly deserted station, it was too late now. When she had bought her ticket and asked to go to the nearest station to Little Pondale, it hadn't even occurred to her to ask how far away Big Whipping was from her destination.

Glancing around, there was nothing big about Big Whipping. The tiny wooden building, painted dark green, with the words 'Ticket Office' painted in white, looked more like a garden shed, and a 'Closed' sign dangled on a piece of string, hanging from a hook. There were no taxis waiting in the equally tiny car park. Not that she could probably afford a taxi after splashing out on a day return ticket for the train. And losing a ten quid T-shirt.

It didn't look as though there were any buses either. As far as the eye could see in any direction there was nothing but one country lane, several empty fields and an abundance of trees and hedges.

She didn't even know in which direction Little Pondale was. This didn't bode well for her apology. She had no alternative but to phone Mia on her landline and ask for directions. Except there didn't seem to be any phone signal. Perhaps it wasn't only Little Pondale that was bereft of mobile phone reception.

But maybe there was hope. A red van was tearing down the lane towards her. Perhaps she could wave it down and ask for assistance. She dashed forward but was surprised when the driver indicated and turned into the empty car park. He stopped in front of a concrete post, and Breanna noticed that affixed to it was a small, red post-box. Then she saw the Royal Mail logo on the side of the van.

'Excuse me,' she said, racing towards the postman. 'Could you tell me how I get to Little Pondale from here, please?'

He opened the box and emptied two letters into his sack, giving her a quick smile. 'From here? On foot?' He shook his head and whistled. 'Over the fields would be your best bet.' He glanced down at her shoes, slinging the virtually empty sack over his shoulder like a slim, beardless, but equally ancient, Father Christmas. 'But not in those heels. And it's a good five miles down the lane. Whereabouts in Little Pondale are you headed?'

'Little Pond Farm. I tried to call but I couldn't get a signal.'

He smiled. 'No mobile reception in these parts. They don't know you're coming?'

Breanna shook her head and shrugged. 'It was a spur of the moment decision.'

He laughed. 'I've had those. That's how I married the wife.' He tossed the sack in the back of the van, slammed the doors and, still chuckling, opened the driver's door. 'Well, come on then. Don't just stand there like a wilting willow. Or do I mean weeping?' He shrugged. 'Whatever. Get in. But don't tell the powers that be, or you'll get me fired. I've got to make a couple of stops along the way, but I'll get you to Little Pond Farm. And a lot faster than if you walked.'

Breanna couldn't believe her luck as she scrambled into the passenger seat. 'Thank you so, so much. That's really kind. I'm Breanna. It's lovely to meet you.'

'I'm Billy.' He smiled as he started the engine. 'So are you a friend of Jet's or Mia's?'

'Mia's. At least, I hope I still am.'

By the time Billy dropped Breanna at the front door of Little Pond Farm, with a handful of mail for Mia and Jet, she had told him all about her lie and what had happened in the bridal shop yesterday.

He had told her about virtually everyone who lived in Little Pondale; about the previous vicar and his nefarious ways; about Matilda Ward, Mia's great-aunt, and how he wasn't in the least bit surprised when he learnt the woman had been a spy in the Second World War, or that she was loaded. He even told Breanna about Alexia Bywater and her return to Lily Pond Lane, and lastly, and most importantly as far as Breanna was concerned, about Garrick Swann and the tragic and sudden death of his partner Fiona who was the mother of his baby, Flora.

Breanna had heard a little bit about Fiona, Garrick and Flora from Mia and Ella, yesterday, but neither of them had seemed eager to talk about the tragedy or how Garrick was coping now that he had moved back to Lily Pond Lane. Certainly not as eager as Billy had been. Although hearing that Billy didn't think it would be long before the beautiful Alexia put a permanent smile back on Garrick's face was information Breanna could have happily done without.

It may have been almost twenty-eight years since Breanna had planted that smacker of a kiss on Garrick's mouth, but even now, just the mention of his name made her unconsciously lick her lips.

Chapter Seven

Mia wasn't sure what astonished her the most when she opened the door of Little Pond Farm. That Billy, who tooted his horn and waved before speeding off down the drive, had delivered the mail before eleven-thirty in the morning, or that Breanna Wright was standing on the doorstep, holding a pile of letters in her hand.

'Bree?'

'Hello Mia. I hope you don't mind me turning up unannounced. If it's not convenient I can come back later.'

Mia looked around but the only vehicles in the drive belonged to her, Jet, Franklin and Pete.

'Er. No.' Mia shook her head. 'It's fine. But how did you get here?'

Breanna glanced over her shoulder at Billy's disappearing brake lights and smiled. 'By train. Billy took pity on me at the station and gave me a lift. I assumed there would be a bus or something.'

Mia shook her head again. 'No. The only way to get from the station is by car or taxi. Well, that's not quite true. There is a bus but it only runs first thing in the morning and first thing in the evening. It's for commuters. Not that anyone uses it to commute. What are you doing here? Sorry. Come in.' She stepped aside to let Breanna pass.

'Wow.' Breanna scanned the spacious hall, her eyes wide, her mouth open. 'This is beautiful.'

Mia smiled. 'It is. Come into the kitchen and I'll make some coffee.'

'Thanks. I could murder a cup. I missed my first one this morning.' She followed Mia into the kitchen and took a seat at the table as Mia indicated.

'Did you get my message? I was a bit concerned that I haven't heard from you. I thought something may have happened.'

Breanna sighed. 'Another disaster, you mean?'

'No. Well maybe.' Mia filled the kettle. 'Is instant fine or would you prefer fresh?'

'Instant's fine. With milk, please. No sugar.'

Mia switched on the kettle and busied herself getting mugs, and the milk from the fridge. Neither she nor Breanna spoke for several seconds. The kettle clicked off and after making the coffee, Mia took a seat at the table, passing one mug to her guest.

Breanna clasped her hands around the mug, took one long gulp and sighed again before putting the mug back on the table and taking a deep breath. 'That's why I'm here. No. Don't worry.

Not because there's been another disaster. I'm here because of yesterday. I'm really sorry, Mia, and there's no excuse at all. I know that. But the truth is, I lied. I don't have a business. I'm not a wedding planner. I work full time in Sainsbury's.'

Mia met her look and could see that Breanna was genuinely sorry.

'That's what Ella said.'

Breanna frowned. 'I'm sorry? Ella knew I'd lied?'

Mia nodded. 'She's brighter than she looks.' She threw Breanna a reassuring grin. 'So why did you lie?'

'I honestly don't know.' Breanna shook her head. 'No. That's not true. I do know.' She sighed yet again. 'I didn't want you, your mum, and more importantly, Ella to think I was some saddo looking at wedding dresses when I don't even have a boyfriend. But that's exactly what I was doing. It sounds ridiculous, I know. But it makes me happy. I do it all the time.' She gave a little laugh. 'I'm running out of shops to go to. I always hoped that by the time I did the circuit again, the sales assistants would either have changed, or would've forgotten me. And over the years, it seems to have worked. You know that all I ever dreamt about at school was being a wedding planner and having my own business. When I saw you standing there, it just popped into my head. And the stupid thing is, it didn't even occur to me for one second that the reason you were there was because you were going to look at wedding dresses for a genuine reason. That you were getting married. And it definitely didn't occur to me that you might want a wedding planner. I'm really sorry, Mia. I know we've lost touch over the years, and everything, but I still think of you and Ella as friends, and I couldn't leave things the way they were.'

Mia fiddled with the handle of her coffee mug. 'You could've told me all this over the phone.'

Breanna nodded. 'I know. And I don't know why I didn't. I have no idea what made me get off the bus and get on a train. Perhaps if I'd known the station was so far away from you, I would've thought twice. Especially as I've got a shift at Sainsbury's this evening. But I suppose that's me, isn't it? I never think before I speak or act. I just jump right in and hope for the best. You'd think I would've learnt my lesson by now. But I couldn't leave things as they were and I suppose I felt you deserved to be told the truth, face to face.'

Mia didn't answer right away, and Breanna quickly emptied her mug and got to her feet. Mia reached out a hand and grabbed Breanna's sleeve.

'I'm glad you got on that train. I'm glad you came here.'

'So am I. But now I'll leave you in peace. Thanks for the coffee. And thanks again for yesterday. There was no way I could've afforded to pay for all that damage. And thanks for wanting to be a client. I just wish I had a wedding-planning business. But the sad fact is, I don't, and I never will. Especially now I've got to move. I realised yesterday, before I went into that shop, that I've got to put those dreams behind me and get on with real life.'

That last sentence sounded sad and hopeless and as Mia watched Breanna turn to walk away, her heart went out to her, especially so when Breanna added: 'I hope you have a wonderful wedding, Mia, and a fabulously happy future.'

'Excuse me,' Mia said. 'Where do you think you're going? My mum's wonderful, and Ella's fantastic, but if I listen to them, and all the other people in this village, my wedding really will turn into a disaster. I need all the help I can get, believe me. What do you say, Bree? Will you be my wedding planner?'

The look on Breanna's face showed just how incredulous she was. 'But … I'm not a wedding planner. I don't have a business, Mia. I work in Sainsbury's.'

Mia shrugged. 'Yes. So you said. Isn't it possible to do both? Although, it seems to me, that if you really want to be a wedding planner and have your own business, you should go for it. It's important for us all to pursue our dreams.'

'Believe me, Mia. Nothing would make me happier. But, sadly I don't have the money to do that. I need to work to pay my bills.' Breanna hurriedly sat back down and leant forward, her fingers clasped, prayer-like, her eyes alight with excitement. 'But if you're truly serious. I mean, if you're actually willing to take a chance on me, I could do both. I'm sure I could. I'll work every evening, every weekend, every spare minute when I'm not at Sainsbury's, I promise. And I promise I won't let you down.'

Mia smiled. 'I'm sure you won't. I've got a good feeling about this. Meeting in that shop was Fate. I know it was. Hold on a minute.' Mia got to her feet and dashed towards the door leading out to the farmyard. 'Stay there. Don't move. Unless you want to make yourself another mug of coffee. In which case, help yourself. I'll be back before you know I've gone.' She raced outside and searched for Jet, calling his name as she ran.

'What's happened?' He appeared from the chicken barn, a concerned look on his face.

'Nothing bad,' Mia said, laughing and breathless. 'It's good. It's all good. At least I think it is. You know I told you about meeting an old friend, Bree, yesterday, and that she was a wedding planner, except Ella didn't believe she was, and that she hadn't returned my call. Bree, not Ella.'

Jet laughed. 'I may be getting older, but I'm not senile yet. I can remember what you told me last night. So what's the good news? That Ella was wrong, and your friend Bree genuinely is a wedding planner?'

Mia shook her head. 'No. Ella was right. Bree lied. Because she was embarrassed. She's not

49

wedding planner. Well, not yet. But she's always wanted to be. And she could be. I'm sure she could. So here's the thing. How would you feel about us investing in a wedding-planning business?'

Jet blinked several times. 'A wedding-planning business? Let me get this straight. A friend you haven't seen for years causes God knows how much damage in a shop, which you pay for, then she lies to you, and you want to give her money to start the business that she told you she has, but didn't really have? Is that right? What's suddenly made you come to this decision?'

'Bree. She's in the kitchen. She caught a train, to come here and say she's sorry. She was standing on our doorstep with our mail in her hand. Billy gave her a lift from the station.'

'Wait. What? No, forget it. She's in the kitchen. Our kitchen?'

'Yes.' Mia nodded. 'What is wrong with you this morning? You're not usually this confused.'

His eyes opened wide. 'Really? Because from where I'm standing, I've been nothing but confused since the day I met you. Confused, and in love, of course.'

'But not confused about being in love? Please say you're not confused about that.'

He smiled lovingly and pulled her into his arms. 'No. Not a bit confused about that. Absolutely, one hundred and ten per cent certain about that.' He kissed her to prove his point, and after, said: 'So, your friend is in our kitchen, and you've come to ask me if I'm happy for you to give her money to start a business she's always dreamt of owning? Yes?'

'Yes.'

'Just one thing. Did she ask you for the money? Or was it your idea?' He laughed and shook his head. 'I think I know the answer but I just want to be sure.'

'She didn't ask. She genuinely only came to apologise. But it makes perfect sense to me. And I think it's Fate.'

His lips twitched into his usual gorgeous smile. 'Of course you do. And who am I to argue with Fate? I know what it's like to have a dream, and if not for Mattie, my dream would never have become a reality. It's your money, Mia. You can do what you like with it. But thank you for asking me. I love you. And it seems you're going to be a partner in a wedding-planning business.'

Mia smiled and kissed him on the lips. '*We're* going to be partners in a wedding-planning business, Jet. Because as I keep telling you, my money is your money. But we're going to be silent partners, okay?'

'Absolutely. And I'm assuming this means that we'll be silent partners planning our own wedding. Confused? Me?'

He laughed and returned her kiss until, several seconds later, she gently eased him away.

'I've left Bree in the kitchen. She'll be wondering where I am. Come and meet her. We can give her the good news together. Over lunch. It's almost noon. And then I'd better give her a lift back to the station because she needs to get to Sainsbury's.'

'Sainsbury's? Why does she need to get to …? No. I'm not even going to ask.'

He was laughing as Mia grabbed his hand and led him towards the kitchen door.

Chapter Eight

Mia was relieved that Jet and Breanna liked one another right away, and the three of them spent a couple of hours chatting. And not merely about the wedding-planning business. Jet also had some news which he shared over their extended lunch, and because of that, Mia had even more good news to tell her mum and Ella.

After dropping an ecstatically happy, Breanna at the station in time for her to catch the three-thirty train to London, Mia called in on both Lori and Ella to ask them to join her for a celebratory glass of wine or two, refusing to say why, until they were comfortably seated in the sitting room at Little Pond Farm.

Ella and Lori, who were sitting beside one another on the sofa, looked equally astonished when Mia explained the reasons for her excitement.

'It's definitely Fate,' Mia said, after pouring the wine and opening a box of cakes she'd bought from Lake's Bakes while waiting for Ella to get ready. She hadn't wanted to wait in Sunbeam Cottage. She and Jet may have agreed to forget 'that business with Garrick' but Mia felt it was a bit too soon to be popping in to the place where Garrick was living. 'It's all such perfect timing. Not only is Bree going to finally be starting *The Wright Wedding*, she's going to be starting it from here.'

'From here?' Ella glanced at Lori over the rim of her wine glass as Mia shoved a massive chocolate éclair in front of her on a plate. 'From Little Pond Farm?'

'Yes. I wanted her to stay and celebrate with us, but she has a shift at Sainsbury's this evening, so she had to get back. Well no. Actually not from here, exactly. From one of the cottages on the farm.'

Lori put her glass on the side table next to her and gave Mia an anxious look, completely ignoring the doughnut oozing with jam and fresh cream, on the plate Mia held out to her.

'Which cottage, exactly?'

'Oh don't worry, Mum. She won't be your neighbour. I didn't know this until today because Ben's daughter only told Jet this morning, but Ben's moving out and going to live with his daughter and her family in Surrey.'

'Ben?' Ella asked, her mouth half full of éclair. 'Who's Ben?'

'You know Ben,' Lori said, flicking Ella's arm with her fingers before grabbing the plate and the cream-laden doughnut. 'Ben Wantage.'

'O-oh. OldBenwherecouldhebe, you mean? The guy who supposedly walks around dressed like a Jedi Knight but who no one ever sees.'

Mia grinned. 'That's the one. Although Jet says Ben actually thinks he's a Black Friar. That's a religious order otherwise known as the Dominicans or something. He used to work on the farm before Jet owned it, but he retired due to ill health, shortly after Jet took over. He's lived in the cottage since he was a boy, and Jet would never ask him to leave. But his mental faculties have seriously deteriorated to such a degree that a daily carer's no longer sufficient. Ben's daughter has decided it's time he went to live with them and she gave Jet notice this morning.'

Ella frowned. 'So Bree's going to use the place as her business premises? That's a long way to come to run a business. Oh hold on.' The frown grew more pronounced. 'Are you telling us that Bree is moving down to Little Pondale?'

'You've got it in one,' Mia said, grinning broadly. 'It makes perfect sense. She's got to move out of her mum's house. She'd planned to move in with a friend, temporarily, but what's the point? If she's going to be planning my wedding anyway, she may as well be close by. And with the internet et cetera, it doesn't matter where she runs her business from. She's going to give in her notice at

Sainsbury's today, and because she's owed so much holiday, she thinks they'll take that into account. She could be here by the end of next week. Ben's moving out on Thursday, so Jet's going to have the place cleaned ready for Bree to move in. Isn't it exciting?' Mia clapped her hands together.

Ella grabbed the wine bottle from the coffee table and topped up their three glasses. 'That's one word for it. I seriously hope Jet's got the cottage insured. Because we know Bree. She'll probably, accidentally burn the place down.'

Lori laughed and shook her head. 'You shouldn't joke about such things, Ella. But I'll admit the poor girl does seem a little more accident-prone than most people.'

'Accident-prone?' Ella shrieked. 'I think that's the understatement of the year.'

Mia tutted. 'Oh come on. That's not fair. We haven't seen her for years. Yesterday was probably a one-off. She was fine at lunch. Well, she did spill coffee over the kitchen table – but that was because she was so excited when Jet and I said we were going to help her start her business, and even more so when we told her she could move in to Willow Cottage, so that was why she also dropped the cup. Anyway. Let's give her a chance. Let's have a toast to Bree and to *The Wright Wedding*. Oh, and to my wedding being Bree's first, complete success.'

'I'll drink to that.' Ella clinked her glass against Mia's as she raised it in the air.

'Cheers.' Lori also raised hers. 'To Bree, *The Wright Wedding*, and to Mia having the wedding of her dreams.'

'Let's hope Bree doesn't turn it into a nightmare,' said Ella, knocking back her wine in several large gulps.

Chapter Nine

Madeleine Wright seemed blissfully happy when Breanna broke the news to her, but a week later, when the removal van arrived to take Breanna's few belongings to her new home, there were tears in Madeleine's eyes.

'Oh please don't cry, Mum. You'll be moving in a couple of weeks anyway, and it's not as if I'll be a million miles away. Plus, the best bit is that the cottage has two bedrooms. You can come and stay whenever you like. Oh, and I didn't tell you, did I? I'll even be getting a car. Nothing fancy or anything. But a car, Mum. Mia told me yesterday when she called. I keep wanting to pinch myself because this is all so wonderful that I'm sure it must be a dream and I'll wake up and find that I'm late for work at Sainsbury's.'

Madeleine smiled and hugged Breanna tight before looking her in the eye. 'I'm so happy for you, my darling. It's about time you had a lucky break. I know we both agreed that me moving into the retirement village made sense for both of us, but if I'm honest, I was worried about you. Especially about you living alone in a room in someone else's house. I don't want you to let your life slip by. I want you to enjoy it. To live it to the full. And it finally sounds as if that may be happening. Now you just have to trust in yourself and do your best. I haven't seen Lori or her daughter for years, but I do remember them being lovely people. And Lori and I still exchange Christmas cards. I'm sure they'll take good care of you.'

Breanna laughed. 'I'm thirty-four, Mum. A grown woman. I can take care of myself.'

Madeleine gave her a doubtful look. 'You'd think so, wouldn't you? But sometimes I worry.' She brushed Breanna's cheek with her fingers, leant forward and kissed her daughter's forehead. 'Now I know you said that mobile phone reception is non-existent, but is there a landline I can call you on? I'll need to know you're safe and happy.'

Breanna nodded. 'Yes. There's a landline. Jet said he'd arrange to have the number transferred into my name, so it should remain the same.' She scribbled the number on a notepad and also texted it to Madeleine's mobile phone. 'If it has to change, I'll call you with the new number. Thanks for letting me take some of the furniture. Mia said they'd sort out anything I needed, but they've done so much, and been so kind, it's good that I can actually turn up with all my bedroom furniture, a sofa, a table and chairs, and a few other things besides.'

Madeleine smiled. 'I wish I could let you have it all, my darling. Or better still, give you money to buy new things. But sadly, even with the proceeds from the sale of this house, there won't be much left after the purchase of my new home goes through.' She took Breanna's hands in hers. 'But there will be some money. Not much. Just enough give you a little cushion to fall back on. I won't say, if things don't work out, because I know they will. I feel it in my bones. It'll be a cushion for you to relax on. Let's just say that.'

'Oh, Mum. Now I'm the one who's starting to cry.'

They hugged one another for some time, until one of the removal men said they were ready to leave whenever Breanna was. They were kindly giving her a lift to her new home, in the passenger seat of their van.

'I'll call you as soon as I arrive.' Breanna let Madeleine's fingers slip through her own. 'And I'll see you in two weeks, to help you move.'

She gave her mum a final kiss, then turned and waved and clambered up into the front of the van, ready to start her new adventure.

Ready to live her dream.

Chapter Ten

Mia and Ella were waiting inside Willow Cottage for Breanna to arrive.

'Welcome to your new home!' Mia held a bottle of champagne in one hand and a helium balloon with the same greeting in the other.

Breanna's hand shot to her chest, the key Mia had given her the other day when they met up in London still in the lock and the door only half opened.

'God! You gave me such a fright. But thank you. What a wonderful surprise.'

Ella held the glasses which clinked together as she shook them in the air. 'Welcome to Willow Cottage. Can we open the bubbly now? Or do we have to wait until you've got your things unpacked?'

Mia threw Ella a reprimanding look. 'Let the girl get inside before you try and get her drunk. Oops. That didn't come out right.' She giggled, put the bottle on the small mantelpiece, let the balloon find its own level and gave Breanna a hug. 'This is going to be such fun. I just know it is.'

Ella stood the glasses beside the bottle and she too, hugged Breanna. 'It's going to be an adventure. I'm pretty sure of that.'

Breanna swiped her hand across her cheek and blinked a couple of times, sniffing slightly as she did so. 'I can't believe I'm here. I still can't believe this is happening.'

'I feel the same.' Ella glanced at Mia and smiled.

'Can we get started, Bree?' One of the removal men, who wasn't at all bad looking, stood just outside the door, peering in.

Breanna turned. 'Oh yes, of course. Do you want us to get out of the way?'

He grinned. 'Don't worry, Bree. We'll work around you.'

'Ooh!' Ella said. 'Bree, is it? On first name terms already? He's quite dishy.'

'Is he? I hadn't noticed. I think I'm too excited. But you know me. I still tell everyone my life story within half an hour of meeting them. Whether they want to hear it or not.'

'I didn't know if you had curtains.' Mia smiled and pointed to the sash windows where she'd hung a pair of navy, velveteen curtains. 'These were in the linen cupboard at the farm, and the ones upstairs were Mattie's. If you've got your own, we can replace them, but if not, I hope these will do until you've settled in and decided what you want.'

Breanna smiled. 'I've got the curtains from my bedroom. They match my floral bedding. But other than that, no. I didn't even think about curtains. And neither did Mum, so thank you.'

'And towels?' Mia asked.

'I've got towels, and tea towels, thanks.'

Ella grinned. 'Have you got a kettle? Because if we can't open the bubbly yet, then we may as well have some coffee. I'm sure the removal guys wouldn't say no to that.'

She was right. They echoed an emphatic, 'Yes please,' when Breanna asked them, and the box marked, 'kettle, mugs, drinks and biscuits,' was the first one they brought in.

Mia made the coffee and handed round the mugs, while Ella and Breanna started unwrapping the packed items in the box marked 'sitting room', even though there was nowhere as yet to put anything.

'Jet, and Ella's boyfriend Gill will be here in half an hour or so,' Mia said. 'They'll help to change the curtains, put furniture together, move heavy stuff, or whatever else you need. Do you want to have a look around while we wait for the furniture to be brought in?'

Breanna nodded and smiled. 'I've been dying to. But I didn't want to ask. I know you emailed me some photos, but it's not the same as seeing it for real. This room, for example, is bigger than it looked in the photo.'

Ella laughed. 'Well, it couldn't be much smaller, could it?'

Mia slapped Ella's arm. 'It's a tiny cottage. A workman's cottage. They're all this small. Mum and Franklin's is the same size.'

'Is it? Theirs looks bigger.' Ella glanced around as if she didn't believe Mia.

'Well, it isn't.' Mia smiled at Breanna. 'I'm sorry it's not much.'

'Not much? Sorry. I didn't mean to shriek.' Breanna laughed and shook her head. 'It's wonderful, Mia. Don't forget, I was going to be moving to one room in a shared house. Here, I've got this delightfully cosy sitting room, a surprisingly large kitchen, by the look of it, two bedrooms and a bathroom. What more could I possibly want or need?'

'Personally, I'd want a tall, hunky, gorgeous man as well,' Ella said. 'But that's just me.'

'Oh God, yes. Give me one of those and I'd die happy.'

'Where d'you want me to stick this, love?' The dishy removal man held a standard lamp in one hand and a box marked 'Bedding' balanced in the other.

Breanna glanced at Mia and Ella and the three of them burst out laughing.

'Sorry.' Breanna was the first to control herself. 'The lamp goes in here. The box goes upstairs, please. Either room will do. I haven't picked a room yet.'

He gave her an odd look. 'Right you are.'

They giggled again as he brushed past each of them and headed for the stairs in the corner of the sitting room, depositing the lamp in front of a little side window on the way.

It didn't take long for the two men to unload Breanna's belongings, even taking into account a couple of breaks for more coffee and biscuits and by the time Jet and Gill arrived in Jet's car, the removal van had been gone for ten minutes.

'What took you so long?' Mia was at the door as Jet got out of his car.

He threw her one of his devilish grins. 'Would you believe traffic?'

Mia laughed. 'No. But I would believe you and Gill popped into the pub for a pint.'

Jet gasped as he walked towards her and so did Gill, who said: 'We did no such thing. It was actually Hettie's fault. She said she'd called round to see Flora, but it was pretty obvious she wanted the low-down on Breanna.'

They stepped inside Willow Cottage and Mia introduced Gill to Breanna.

'I'm pleased to meet you, Breanna,' Gill said, holding out his hand in a somewhat formal greeting.

Ella tutted. 'He'll never change. Almost five months living with me and I still haven't knocked the 'posh' out of him.' She raised her eyes skyward and laughed.

'One of us has to have some manners,' Gill replied, trying but failing to suppress his laughter.

Breanna took his hand and shook it. 'I'm very pleased to meet you too. But please, call me Bree. All my friends do.'

'And no jokes about cheese.' Ella wagged a finger at him. 'I'm the joker in this relationship.'

'Yeah right.' Gill smiled at Breanna. 'Ignore her. I do. Oh, shit. I forgot the pizza.'

'What were you saying about manners?' Ella yelled after him as he dashed back towards Jet's car.

Jet shook his head and laughed. 'Gill. You'll need these.' He tossed the keys to Gill, turned back and slipped an arm around Mia. 'He made pizza. That's really why we're late. But Hettie did turn up about five minutes before we left and in our haste to get away, we both forgot the pizza.'

'You went inside Sunbeam Cottage?' Mia tried to sound casual.

Jet grinned. 'I did.'

'Oh God,' said Ella, slumping into one of the chairs beside the table in the middle of the sitting room where the removal men had left it. 'Does my brother have a broken nose? Is he alive?'

Breanna made a strange sound. A cross between a gasp and a soft scream. And all eyes turned to her. She blushed crimson and muttered. 'Sorry. Er. I don't understand. Don't you get on?

Not that it's any of my business. Sorry.' She turned away and fiddled with a couple of candlesticks that had replaced the bottle and glasses on the mantelpiece.

'It's okay,' Mia said. 'Ella was joking. I hope.' She glanced at Jet. 'I'm assuming Garrick's alive. But does he have a broken nose?'

Jet's grin grew wider. 'Not from me. We didn't pop into the pub for a pint, but Gill, Garrick and I did have a beer, and Garrick and I had a long chat while Gill was making the pizzas.' He pulled Mia closer and looked into her eyes. 'And I think I can safely say we've reached an understanding.'

'So you're friends again?' she ventured.

He nodded and kissed her briefly on the lips. 'We're friends again.'

Ella jumped to her feet. 'Thank God for that. Well, it's definitely time for bubbly. We put it in the fridge to chill.' She glanced at Breanna, who was looking rather relieved. 'Shall I do the honours, or you? It's your new home, after all.'

Breanna smiled. 'No. You can do it, if you don't mind. I'm feeling a little emotional all of a sudden. Oh! And I promised I'd call my mum.'

Jet nodded towards the landline phone balanced on the windowsill. 'It's connected. And it's the same number that I told you, if you want to give it to your mum. Shall we go into the kitchen?'

'No. It's fine. Please stay where you are. I'm not going to tell Mum anything I wouldn't want any of you to hear.'

Breanna dialled the number and spoke to her mum, while Ella went into the kitchen to get the bubbly and retrieve the glasses.

Mia looked into Jet's eyes. 'Have I told you lately how much I love you, Jet Cross?'

He gave her a thoughtful look but the corners of his mouth twitched. 'I don't believe you have. Not since breakfast anyway.'

She grabbed him by his jacket collar and pulled him to her, kissing him as if they were the only people in the room, until Ella said: 'Can't you two keep your hands off one another?'

'Apparently not,' said Jet, grinning broadly when he and Mia parted. 'It's a good thing we're getting married.'

'It's a very good thing.' Mia nodded her head, her gaze still firmly fixed on Jet.

A screech of tyres and the slam of a car door announced Gill's return and Ella opened the door just as Breanna said goodbye to her mum and hung up the phone.

'I'm back,' Gill said, red-faced and a little breathless, carrying three large, pizza-sized, plastic containers. 'I made a few, because I didn't know what Breanna, sorry Bree, liked.'

'I like anything. Thank you. You made these yourself?'

Gill smiled. 'I enjoy cooking.'

Ella grinned. 'And I enjoy watching him cook. We've got the perfect relationship.'

'Open the champagne, Ella,' Mia said. 'Have you got some plates, Bree?'

'Plates. Yes. Somewhere.' She dashed into the kitchen and a few seconds later returned with a stack of plates and a roll of kitchen towel. 'They were washed before they were packed, so they should just need wiping over.'

But as she said it, she stumbled over the corner of a rug which hadn't been laid quite flat, and the plates slipped from her grasp, smashing to smithereens on the solid oak floorboards before anyone had time to catch them.

'Oh no.' Mia hurried to her and wrapped an arm around her shoulder while Jet bent down to pick up the pieces, and Ella put the bottle and glasses on the table and went in search of a dustpan and brush. 'I hope they weren't expensive.'

Breanna shook her head. 'No. But they were the only dinner plates I've got.'

'Have you got tea plates?' Gill asked, and Breanna nodded.

Ella handed the dustpan and brush to Jet. 'I'll get them, Bree. You sit down. You've had a long day.' She gave Mia one of her 'I told you so' looks before hurrying back into the kitchen, returning moments later with a stack of tea plates which she kept as far away from Breanna as she possibly could.

Gill placed the containers on the table while Jet finished tidying up. Ella duly popped the cork on the champagne, filled the glasses and handed them round.

'To Bree,' Mia said, raising her glass in the air. 'Here's to you finding happiness, friendship, and love in your new home, and to great success with your new business.'

Everyone cheered and repeated the toast, and Breanna looked as if she would burst into tears.

'Thank you all so much. But mainly, thank you Mia and Jet for your kindness and your friendship and most of all, for your faith and trust in me. And for giving me such a wonderful, and unbelievable opportunity. I promise I won't let you down.'

'We know you won't,' said Jet, raising his glass and smiling reassuringly.

'Just stay away from the crockery,' said Ella, but only loud enough for Mia to hear.

Chapter Eleven

Breanna had never felt so alone in her life.

The day had been exciting but equally tiring; the evening had been fun, but a little embarrassing. First she had made that ridiculous squeal when Ella had mentioned Jet hitting Garrick, and then she had smashed all those plates in front of everyone. She had thought her luck had changed, but clearly some of her bad luck had followed her to Willow Cottage.

Or perhaps it wasn't anything to do with luck. Perhaps today had simply been because she was tired and also rather emotional. She had lived with her mum her entire life. And while she would have had to face the separation when her mum moved, it seemed even more raw because she had been the one to move away. Plus, instead of moving into a shared house in the midst of the hustle and bustle of the London suburbs, she was now living alone in a cottage in the middle of nowhere.

Once everyone had left, she phoned her mum again.

'The cottage is beautiful, Mum. And really cosy. The front door opens directly into the sitting room, but it's a lovely room. So bright and far more spacious than the photos I showed you. There're two fairly large windows either side of the door, and another two small windows on each side wall. There's a flight of stairs leading off the sitting room, and there's a door at the foot of it which you can close to keep out draughts. The sitting room leads directly into the kitchen and there's a utility room, effectively beneath the stairs. Oh, and there's a mantelpiece above a fireplace which has a wood burning stove. Jet said that my closest neighbour, Pete, who works on his farm, will make sure I've always got plenty of wood. Everyone has been so fantastic. Gill, Ella's boyfriend, made pizzas. Mia brought a bottle of champagne and then we drank wine that Gill had brought. It's been the perfect moving day.'

'Then why do I detect a hint of sadness, my darling?'

'Because I miss you, Mum. And now that everyone's left, I feel so alone. It's silly, I know. All I need is a good night's sleep. I'm tired, that's all.'

'I miss you too, my darling. Even more than I thought I would. But it won't be long until I see you. In the meantime, you've got lots to do. I know you'll make me proud, Breanna. And your father too. Wherever he may be. Now get some sleep. Call me tomorrow. I love you. Pleasant dreams, my darling girl.'

'Same to you, Mum. I love you too.'

Breanna hung up and looked around the room. Everyone had helped to unpack and to put things where she wanted them, but there was still a lot to do before she would feel settled.

A high-pitched scream turned her blood to ice, and terrified, she couldn't move.

And then she remembered what Mia and Ella had told her about the foxes and the other wildlife.

'It's just a vixen calling to her mate,' Breanna said to herself, her hand on her heart trying to steady her breathing.

She jumped again.

'And that was the hoot of an owl. Good God, girl. Get a grip. You're living in the country now.'

But the third noise really frightened her. Those were footsteps scrunching on the patch of gravel just outside the door.

'Don't be ridiculous, Bree. Perhaps one of them forgot something.'

She edged her way to the window, moved the curtain slightly and peered into the darkness. It was pitch black out there. No street lamps, no lights from neighbouring houses because there were no neighbouring houses to be seen; no moon and not even a star in the obviously cloudy sky. No light of any kind. Not even a torch. So how could there be footsteps? How could anyone see?

'Oh God.' She rushed to the phone and was about to dial Mia's number when something rapped against the door. She frantically scanned the room; her terror-filled eyes spotted the empty champagne bottle. She grabbed the neck and with shaking limbs forced herself forwards. She hadn't heard a car, so it definitely wasn't Mia or anyone.

The rap came again. Louder this time.

'I've got a weapon,' she wailed. 'And I'm not afraid to use it.'

With a thumping heart and quivering body she yanked the door open, holding the champagne bottle aloft, ready to bring it soundly down on her assailant's head if necessary.

'What the hell?' A tall, agile man jumped backwards out of harm's way.

'Who are you? What do you want?'

'It's Garrick, Bree. Garrick Swann. Ella's brother. She forgot her handbag and both she and Gill are far too drunk to drive. She didn't realise until after Jet had dropped them off. Are you okay? Have you lost your voice? Er. I think you can put that bottle down. I swear to you, it's Garrick. I know we haven't seen each other for at least fifteen years. But don't you recognise me even a little bit?'

'G-Garrick? Really? Is it really you?' She peered into the darkness, her rapid heartbeat now nothing to do with fear.

'Yes. It's me.' He stepped forward a little but he was still in the shadows.

She lowered the champagne bottle and stared at it for a second or two before looking back at him. She blinked several times and as he slowly and cautiously stepped closer, into the shaft of light from the sitting room, she stretched out her arm and touched his shoulder with her fingers, snapping them away the moment she felt the leather of his jacket.

'You're real. I'm not imagining it.'

He gave her a questioning look. 'Clearly Ella and Gill weren't the only ones who've had a lot to drink. Are you okay?'

She nodded, her mouth open, her eyes staring at his face.

'Can I come in and get it?'

'Huh? Get what?' She couldn't believe Garrick Swann was standing in front of her after all these years.

'Ella's handbag.'

'Er, yes. Come in. Come in.'

Coming to her senses, she stepped aside to let him in.

'Thanks. It's lovely to see you, but I really can't stop. I've left Flora, my baby, at home. She's safe, of course. Alexia's there. But I don't want to be longer than I have to.' He cast his eyes about the room without even looking in her direction. 'Ah, there it is.' He grabbed Ella's bag from under the table. 'I wouldn't have come except Ella insisted that if I didn't, she would come here on foot. And believe me she…' His voice trailed off and he blinked several times as he finally turned to face her.

She stared at him and smiled. The last time she had seen him was when she was seventeen, and going off to college to sit her A-levels. Mia and Ella both went to a different college and then to university, which Breanna or her mum had not been able to afford. Older now, and even more gorgeous, broader on the shoulders and possibly slightly taller, his hair still sandy brown, his eyes still that incredible hazel, he'd merely improved with age.

She licked her lips, remembering that kiss when she was six.

And he had run away.

But he wasn't running away now.

He wasn't doing anything except standing in the middle of her sitting room, staring at her as if he couldn't quite believe his eyes.

Chapter Twelve

'You've changed.' Garrick looked her up and down.

'You've hardly changed at all.'

He ran a hand through his hair, Ella's bag tucked beneath his other arm. 'I must have. We were in our teens the last time I saw you.'

Breanna nodded. 'I know. I remember. But you haven't.' She blinked and glanced towards the door. 'How did you get here? I didn't hear a car.'

He shook his head. 'Don't laugh. I went to the wrong cottage. I went to Pete's. And when I realised and got back in, the van wouldn't start. Pete's actually looking at it for me right now, but I didn't know what time you'd be going to bed so I thought I'd nip across the field and pick up the bag. Then the battery on my key torch died, and I don't have my mobile because as you probably know, there's no mobile reception here, so I couldn't use the torch on that.' He shrugged and shook his head again. 'I don't suppose you've got a torch I could borrow. I'll bring it back tomorrow.

Or if you're staying up, and Pete's managed to get the van started, I could drop it back tonight. I just need it to see my way across the field. It's as black as pitch out there.'

'I've only got the torch on my phone. But you're welcome to borrow that. You could drop it back tomorrow. Or tonight. Whichever's easier. To tell you the truth, I could use the company. I hadn't realised how quiet it would be down here, or how terrifying the wildlife sounds.'

He looked torn. 'I can't stay. I've got to get back for Flora. Alexia's with her. She's a friend. You could come back with me. Come and stay with us tonight, I mean. If you're scared. If you'd rather not be on your own.'

'No, it's fine. I'm not scared, exactly. Simply a little nervous. Don't worry. I'm just being silly.'

'I can check the windows and the doors are locked, if that would make you feel any happier.'

'It would. A little. Thanks.'

'No problem. I'll start in here, shall I?'

She nodded. 'If you like. Or you could start in my bedroom and work your way down.'

He blinked a couple of times, gave a little cough, ran a hand through his hair once again and tossed Ella's bag on the table.'

'I'll do that. Which one's your bedroom?'

She smiled. 'The one with the bed in it. I've only got one bed. But Mia's kindly offered to get me another, in case my mum, or anyone, wants to stay.'

'Yes. Mia's very kind. And thoughtful, too.'

'Very. And pretty. Beautiful, in fact, don't you think?'

He nodded. 'Yes. Yes she is.'

Breanna bit her lip. 'Oh Garrick, I'm so sorry. I should've said something before. I don't know what's the matter with me. I heard about Fiona. I'm so dreadfully sorry for your loss.'

He met her eyes and held her look. 'Thank you. Sometimes I can't believe it's actually happened. I wake up and expect to see her lying in bed beside me. Sometimes I'm sure I can hear her laugh. Or say my name in that special Scottish lilt she had. Sometimes I even think I can feel her arms around me.' He shook his head and sighed. 'But it's crazy, I know. She's gone. People tell me I'll get over it in time. And I will. I know I will. But it's hard, you know? And Flora's both a godsend and a torment. I love her with all my heart, but sometimes, when I look at her, all I see is Fiona, and my heart breaks all over again. I don't know if I'm coming or going.' He smirked. 'I even kissed Mia on Valentine's Day. Can you believe that? We dated for a while. Fiona and I had broken up, and then she found out she was pregnant, and we got back together. But I loved Mia, too. I still love her, but as a friend. But it's so confusing sometimes. I miss having someone to hold, and being held. I miss kissing someone, and being kissed. I miss cuddling up to a warm body in the middle of the night. I miss sex. Oh God. I wish

I could close my eyes and wake up in the future. I wish it didn't hurt so much. I wish … Oh shit. I'm sorry. I'm so very sorry. I have no idea why I told you all that. I must go.'

'Garrick. I'm glad you told me. If you ever want to talk, about Fiona, or about anything, I'm here. I'm a good listener. I could be a good friend. If you'd like me to be.'

They looked at one another in silence until a vixen screamed in the distance and Garrick seemed to jump.

'I was going to check your locks. I'll do that now.'

'No, Garrick. It's fine. I'm fine. That was a vixen. I've got to get used to these noises if I'm going to live in the country, and I'm a grown woman. I can check my own locks. But thank you.' She took her mobile from her handbag and held it out to him. 'I charged the battery before I left London today, so it should get you back to the van, at least. I hope it's fixed.' She walked to the door and opened it. 'Don't forget Ella's bag.'

He turned back and grabbed it from the table. 'I'd forget my head if it wasn't screwed on. It was lovely to see you, Bree. I'll see you tomorrow.'

'It was lovely to see you too. I'll be at Mia's for part of the day tomorrow, or she may come here. We've got to really crack on with this wedding.'

'Oh yes. Congratulations, by the way. I hear you're starting a business. If you ever need any help or advice on that score, I'm your man. Because I've got my own business, I mean.'

She smiled and nodded. 'Yes, I know. And I knew what you meant. Thank you. I may well take you up on that.'

'Please do. You know where I am.'

'See you tomorrow then. Good night, Garrick.'

'See you tomorrow. Good night. Sleep well.'

She held the door open and watched him go until the beam of light from the torch on her phone faded into the distance. But once or twice she was sure the beam turned back in her direction. Just for a second or two, as if Garrick had turned back to look at her.

Which was ridiculous, of course. Why would he turn back to look at her? Besides, all he'd be able to see was her silhouette in the doorway.

He had run away from her when she was six, telling her he only liked redheads, not girls with hair the colour of soot.

Nothing much had changed it seemed. Because Fiona had definitely been a redhead. And from the pictures of Alexia Bywater that Breanna had seen from her internet search of social media sites, after Mia and also Billy the postman, had let it slip that Garrick and Alexia might soon be an item, Alexia was a redhead too.

And more to the point, Alexia was the one who Garrick had left his baby with tonight. That told Breanna everything she needed to know.

She closed the door, bolted it, and went upstairs to bed.

Chapter Thirteen

Mia poured four cups of coffee.

'Can't you do that quietly?' Ella held her head in her hands, her elbows propped on the kitchen table at Little Pond Farm. 'It sounds like Niagara Falls.'

Mia laughed. 'I've told you a billion times, don't exaggerate. Besides, it's your fault for drinking so much last night.'

'Yeah, yeah. I don't need a lecture from you, thanks very much. I got the full works from Garrick both last night and this morning. God, that man's a killjoy sometimes.'

Lori threw her a sideways glance. 'Well, he has just lost the mother of his child, so I think even you can forgive him that.'

Ella pulled a face. 'Yeah. I keep forgetting. I'm a really horrible person, aren't I?'

Mia tossed her a strip of painkillers and put a glass of water in front of her on the table. 'You're not horrible. You're one of the kindest, most caring people I know. But you are a bit tactless sometimes. And not everybody gets your jokes.'

'Well, thank you. But you're my biggest fan. Bree? What do you think? Am I horrible?'

Breanna looked startled. She had been in a world of her own since the moment she arrived with Lori who had picked her up on the way to Mia and Jet's.

'Er.' She glanced around the room as all eyes looked in her direction. 'No. No, of course not. But I do agree with Mia. Not everybody understands your jokes. Sometimes people may get the wrong impression and think you're being mean.'

Ella lifted her head from her hands and fixed Breanna with a serious stare before her mouth burst into a wide grin. 'You're right, Bree. I must work on that.' She gave her a wink, popped two tablets from the strip and swallowed each in turn. 'I hope these are fast acting because at the moment it feels like all my brain cells are having a party and I haven't been invited. Oh. Which reminds me.' She fiddled in her bag and took out a mobile phone which she pushed across the table to Breanna. 'Garrick gave me this, with his love.'

'His love?' Breanna did a pretty good impression of the cat who thought she'd got the cream, but realised it was sour milk. She gave a strangled laugh. 'Oh I see. One of your jokes. Very funny.'

Ella frowned, glanced at Mia and back at Breanna. 'No it wasn't. That's exactly what he said. When I told him this morning I was coming here to discuss the plans for Mia's wedding with her, Lori and you, he handed me the phone and told me to give it back to you with his love.' She looked at Lori and Mia. 'What's funny about that? Am I missing something?'

Lori smiled knowingly. 'I think perhaps we all are. Is there something you'd like to share with us, Bree?'

Now Breanna had turned into a startled deer. 'No. Nothing. Nothing at all.'

'Oh my God.' Mia looked from Breanna to Ella and Lori, then back to Breanna with more than a hint of laughter mixed with incredulity in her voice. 'Did something happen between you and Garrick last night?' Mia had asked Breanna on the phone earlier, if she had slept well and Breanna had told her about Garrick collecting Ella's bag, and that she'd nearly hit him with the champagne bottle, but that was all she had said.

'No! Nothing. I told you. I lent him my phone because his key torch battery had died.'

Ella sniggered. 'After nearly bashing his brains out with a bottle.'

Breanna gasped. 'Did Garrick say that?'

Ella shook her head then quickly put her palm against her forehead. 'No. Mia did. What? Don't give me that look, Mia. You did tell me. Oh. Wasn't I supposed to say that?'

Mia sighed. 'Remember what I was saying about being tactless?'

Ella grinned. 'Nope. Don't seem to recall that. Oh, for goodness sake. Everybody knows we tell each other everything.' She smiled at Breanna. 'And the fact you tried to kill my brother is hardly State secret stuff, is it? God. Even Jet knows Mia tells me all about their sex life.'

'Ella!' Mia glowered at her.

'Wh-at?'

Mia shook her head, but Lori persisted. 'So, Bree. Back to you and Garrick. It must have been at least seventeen years since you last saw one another? Did it feel like old times, or is there, perhaps, a flicker of interest on either side?'

'Garrick's not in the least bit interested in me. He told me years ago he only likes redheads, and nothing's changed. Besides, he's dating Alexia, isn't he?'

Ella leant forward, her arms crossed in front of her, her elbows on the table. 'Well, well. That was said with real meaning. Dripping with acid, I think. Could it be that Breanna Wright has the hots for my brother? Did I detect more than a hint of resentment and even jealousy in those words?'

Mia slapped her arm. 'Tact, Ella. Tact. Try it.' She smiled at Breanna. 'We understand completely if you'd rather not tell us, but if you like Garrick, that's nothing to be ashamed of, or embarrassed about. And in spite of the way the three of us behave sometimes, my mum included, if you didn't want Garrick to know, he wouldn't hear it from us, I can promise you that.'

Ella frowned at Mia. 'He wouldn't?'

'No, Ella. He would not.'

Ella shrugged. 'Okay, fine.' She grinned at Breanna, who had been decidedly quiet. 'So Bree. Do you want to get my brother into bed?'

Breanna gasped and turned a rather vivid shade of crimson, while Mia tutted, looked at Lori and rolled her eyes in despair.

'If you do,' Ella continued, undaunted, 'you've got my blessing. I know Alexia's changed, and I'm very happy for her, but I still don't like the idea of having her in my family. I'm sorry. That's just the way it is. And some rampant sex would definitely be good for Garrick. Although, perhaps it's best if he does that with Alexia. He's grieving, after all, and if you really like him you don't want to be the rebound girl, do you? So my advice would be, let him mess around with Alexia until he's got his grief out of his system, and you be the girl he goes to when he's returned to his senses.' She smiled triumphantly and flopped back in her chair, the smile fading slightly. 'Now what?'

Lori shook her head. 'I never thought I'd say this, Ella, but I think you've just outdone Hettie in the 'how deep can I put my foot in this?' department.'

Mia coughed. 'Ok-ay. I think if Bree has something to say, she'll tell us when she's ready. So, hastily moving on. Let's talk about my wedding. Bree? Are you ready?'

'Huh?' Bree looked as if she'd been run over by a steam roller. More than once. She blinked, shook her head, took several gulps of coffee then pulled a face, obviously realising it was cold. She cleared her throat, fidgeted in her seat and finally said: 'Yes. I'm ready. Where would you like to start?'

'I'll make some fresh coffee.' Lori's chair scraped against the tiled floor as she stood up.

Mia smiled. 'Good idea, Mum. Um. I think we should start with my dress. Ella suggested I could have one made, and I really like that idea. We've looked through endless bridal magazines and while all the dresses are beautiful, I haven't seen one that really took my breath away. And that's what I want. Well, to take Jet's breath away. But only for a moment, of course. I'd like him to be breathing when he says his vows.'

Ella, who had appeared to be momentarily sulking, sat bolt upright, reached into her bag, and brought out an A4 drawing pad. Flicking a couple of pages, she slid the pad towards the centre of the table while Breanna was nodding at Mia.

'What's that?' asked Lori, leaning over to gather the mugs together.

Ella shrugged. 'It's a sketch I made.'

Mia's eyes opened wide, and so did her mouth. 'Oh, Ella! This is gorgeous. You drew this?'

Ella smiled affectionately at Mia. 'I was taking mental notes of all the things you said you liked and didn't like while we were looking through the magazines. I'm no dress designer, obviously. But I think it sort of gives Bree an idea of the kind of thing you want.'

'It gives her more than an idea. It's damn near perfect.' Mia jumped up, dashed to Ella and hugged her, kissing her loudly and repeatedly in a jokey fashion on her head and cheeks.

'Get off.' Ella pushed her away, laughing.

Breanna pulled the pad closer and studied it. 'I don't have any well-known dress designers on my contacts list, obviously,' she joked. 'But I do have a friend from my yoga class who studied Fashion at Kingston University and got a first class honours degree. Plus, she did a couple of work placements in couture houses in Italy and the US and one with a large fashion company here. I don't know the details because as you can see from the way I dress, fashion's not my thing, but I know lots of people in the yoga class were really impressed. She's only young. In her early twenties, I think, but she is lovely, down-to-earth, and really easy to talk to. I could give her a call if you like. No commitment on either side. Just a friendly chat.'

'You do yoga?' Ella asked.

'You're missing the point, I think,' said Mia, laughing. 'That would be fantastic, Bree. Is she working? If she's with a fashion house, she may not be able to do freelance work.'

Breanna shook her head. 'She's just come back from a gap year. She's been travelling the world, getting ideas, taking notes and meeting people in all aspects of the fashion industry, from a group of women in India who make the most incredible fabrics, apparently to high-end fashion photographers. She's starting her own business, so she wanted to learn as much as she could first hand. Her parents are loaded, so money isn't an issue.'

'Oh. She probably won't be interested in designing a wedding dress for me then. Especially in such a short time frame.'

'There's no harm in asking,' Bree said, glancing at her watch. 'In fact, if I can use your phone, I'll give her a call right now. She jogs first thing, then does a few hours' work, so she should be home.'

'Please do.' Mia nodded towards the phone. 'You can use that one, or, if you'd like some privacy, there's a phone in the sitting room.'

'This one's fine.'

Mia tried not to listen while Breanna discussed her with the young designer called Delphinie, and expected the answer to be no when Breanna said goodbye after merely a few minutes.

'Is she French?' asked Ella. 'Delphinie sounds French. But isn't it Delphine, as in Queen? Not Delphinie as in Bee?'

Breanna giggled. 'She was born in Brixton, but she lives in Chelsea now. Her mum was a model, whose favourite flower's a Delphinium, apparently. Delphinium didn't sound as nice as Delphinie, so the story goes. So it's pronounced as in Bee. Delphinie.'

'Ah,' said Lori, handing Breanna a fresh mug of coffee. 'That's lovely.'

'I'm glad my mum didn't name me after her favourite flower,' Ella said. 'It's Carnation.'

'She said no, didn't she?' Mia let out a deflated sigh.

Breanna shook her head. 'She said she can come down tomorrow. If she's only got three months, the sooner she gets started, the better.'

Mia was astonished. 'She said yes? Just like that?'

'She said that she'll do it, provided she likes you when she meets you tomorrow. And I know that goes without saying, so yes, I'm certain she'll do it.'

'Oh my God!' said Ella. 'You'd better be on your best behaviour then.'

Mia threw her an anxious smile. 'And perhaps you'd better be nowhere in sight. At least until after she's agreed.' She nudged Ella and laughed.

'Actually,' said Ella. 'That's probably not a bad idea.'

'That's the dress sorted, possibly,' said Lori, returning to her seat at the table. 'What's next on the list?'

'Bridesmaids' dresses. But I think we may have found those. At least, Ella's seen one she likes and I emailed a link to Tiffany. Oh, she's Jet's half-sister, Bree, and she's my other bridesmaid. Anyway. She emailed back this morning and said that she liked it too. So provided they're in stock, in the right sizes, that's another thing we can tick off the list.'

'Excellent. And next?' Lori grabbed a biscuit from the barrel on the table.

'The wedding invitations.' Mia went to the dresser and took two boxes from the cupboard. 'I got Fred to design them. I wanted something simple, but cheerful and bright. Not formal white. Jet likes them, so we're going with these. Fred's got a friend in the printing business, who's an absolute star as far as I'm concerned. So's Fred, for that matter. We had quite a few printed, especially as we're bound to make mistakes writing them out. Aren't we, Ella?' She grinned as she put the boxes on the table, removed the lids and everyone peered inside.

'They're lovely,' Ella said.

'But? I could hear a definite 'but' in there.'

'They look more like an invite to a party, than a wedding. I love them. Don't get me wrong. And I'm not just saying that to be nice.'

Mia laughed. 'That's perfect then. Because that's exactly what we're going for. We want this to be a party. A celebration of our love. But neither of us want it to be formal, or too pompous or anything. That's strange, I know, but the more I've thought about this wedding, the more I want it to be fun. And Jet agrees. In fact he's relieved. He thought I'd want the Ritz or something, or helicopters landing on Frog Hill to fly everyone to a castle somewhere. That's his idea of hell. But he'd go along with it and be happy, if that's what I wanted. Except it's not.'

'That sounds like my ideal wedding.' Ella grinned and grabbed a biscuit.

Mia nodded. 'I thought so too. But I've realised it's not what I want at all.' She reached for a biscuit but changed her mind. She'd need to watch her weight from now on. 'What I want is for it to be a happy day for everyone, not just for me and Jet. The church bit will be formal, of course, but the rest of it, I'd like to be more like a birthday party than a wedding. And I want the entire village to be invited to at least some part of it. And to get something. A little gift from me and Jet. A memento. Just something small.'

'Okay,' Breanna said. 'I like the invitations. And the fact that they're not formal sets the perfect tone. It tells people this is going to be fun. A day where, perhaps, anything goes. What if you included the gift with the invitation? All the ones in the village can be hand delivered, can't they? We may have to rethink the ones we need to post, depending on the gift.'

Ella dunked a second biscuit in her coffee. 'What? So even if people don't come to the wedding, they still get a gift?'

Mia nodded. 'Yes. I love that. We'll only be inviting people we actually want, so if they can't come, it'll probably be for a good reason. I'd like them to have a little token of the day, even if they're not there. And I'm not sending cake to anyone. So that's out.'

Breanna looked deep in thought. 'Did you say, your friend Fred's printer can do anything?'

Mia nodded. 'Yes. Why? What are you thinking?'

'Just an idea, but your wedding's at the end of May. What about if we sent everyone a pack of seeds? And had the printers make a special packet for them. With a photo of you and Jet and the date of the wedding on it. Sweet peas, for example. They'd match the invitations. They're a friendly, informal but beautiful and definitely cheerful flower. And they're fast-growing. We could ask people to plant them, in a pot if they don't have a garden, and, assuming they germinate, which could be an issue for someone like me who would probably kill them, but anyway. For those who could keep them alive, we could suggest they might like to cut a few and wear them on the day. Men could wear them as boutonnières. Women could either pin a small bunch to their outfits or add them to their hats, or in their hair. And for those who couldn't attend, they'd have a cheerful reminder of you and Jet and your wedding. It'd be flowering on the day, and possibly for years to come, because once they establish themselves, sweet peas can grow for years.'

'I love it!' Mia clapped her hands together and beamed at everyone.

Lori seemed overjoyed too but Ella looked a little surprised. As if she hadn't expected Breanna to come up with anything useful.

'That's a fantastic idea,' she said. 'Especially as Jet's a farmer. The seeds would represent the shoots of your love. And it has been a bit of a whirlwind romance, so the fact they're fast-growing is also apt. You could even have them in your bouquet. I'll get Gill to grow ours. I'm as bad as Bree when it comes to plants and flowers.'

'That's settled then,' Mia said. 'But where do we get all the seeds from?'

'We could order them.' Breanna typed something into her laptop. The brand new laptop that Mia and Jet had bought her, to help her run her business. 'Yes. There seem to be several places. Or, if you want to keep things local, we could try a garden centre. There must be one nearby. Oh. That's odd. Nothing's coming up.'

'Jet will know. Or Hettie. I'll ask.' Mia made a note.

'Or Billy, the postman,' Breanna added, with a smile. 'He seems to know everything. He even came to Willow Cottage this morning. Just to say hello because he'd heard I'd moved in. Word certainly gets around down here, doesn't it?'

Mia laughed. 'You have no idea. It spreads like wildfire. No one has any secrets for long. Except for Mattie, my great aunt. Not even Billy knew about her.'

Ella gave a little cough. 'So you see, Bree. It's pointless to try and keep anything secret around here. Especially a secret crush. Unless you've been trained by the SOE or MI5 or 6, and you're a super-spy extraordinaire. So if you've got the hots for Garrick, everyone will soon find out. What? I'm only saying.'

Chapter Fourteen

Breanna was feeling pleased with herself. The morning had gone extremely well and Mia seemed genuinely happy with what had been agreed so far. Delphinie and Mia would get on, she had no doubt of that, so the wedding dress could be ticked off the list … in theory. So could the invitations and, unless there were unforeseen problems either obtaining the sweet pea seeds, or having the special covering packets printed, the gift to go with each invitation could also be ticked.

Lori left at lunchtime for a shopping trip with Franklin, but Jet took Lori's seat and Mia filled him in. He was more than pleased with everything and had some news of his own.

'I've spoken to Bear. Oh. He's a friend, Bree and his real name's Rupert, but everyone calls him Bear. We'll explain all that later. Anyway, his friend, Craig who lives in Little Whittingdale was the guy who did the video of Hettie and Fred's wedding and he's told Bear he's happy to do our photos and a video of the day. You don't know

Hettie and Fred yet either, Bree. In fact, I think it'd be a good idea if we took you to The Frog and Lily as soon as possible so you can meet everyone. That way you'll have some idea of who we're talking about.'

'That's an excellent idea,' Mia said. 'I've told Bree a little about everyone, but it would be much better to meet them all in the flesh. What about tonight?'

Jet nodded. 'That's fine with me. Bree? You up for that?'

'Yes. I have no plans other than working on the wedding. That would be great. Um. Would Craig also be able to take the photo we need for the seed packet? We'll need that pretty soon. Like, this coming week really, because we should get the invitations out asap. It's already the 2nd of March and that doesn't give guests much time. The invitations request RSVPs by the 26th.'

'It shouldn't be a problem. I'll speak to Bear and let you know. He'll be in the pub tonight. Which reminds me.' He leant closer to Mia. 'His girlfriend dumped him last night.'

She seemed surprised. 'What? The one he started seeing at Christmas?'

'That doesn't surprise me,' Ella said. 'He's a bit … over eager.'

'Is he?' Jet tucked into his bowl of pasta.

'Well, he was all over Mia like a rash, and they only dated for a couple of days.'

Jet threw her a sardonic smile. 'Thanks for reminding me.'

Mia playfully slapped his arm. 'Oh come on. You know full well that nothing happened between me and Bear. But Ella's right. He was a bit OTT. Desperate, almost.'

Jet pulled a face. Something between regret and sympathy. 'Personally, I think the guy still has a thing for Alexia, but he won't admit it.'

'Alexia?' Bree almost choked on a piece of chicken in her pasta.

Ella grinned. 'Alexia's dated everyone in Little Pondale. And probably the surrounding areas. With the possible exception of Fred. But he's in his eighties, so he's not really her type. She even dated Garrick for a couple of weeks, but he dumped her for Mia. Although they seem pretty friendly again right now. This village is a hotbed of lust, you know. If you're looking for a man, this is the place to be.'

Mia pressed Jet. 'What makes you think Bear still has a thing for Alexia?'

He grinned. 'By the way he looks at her, especially when he thinks no one else is watching. And the fact that he never talks about her.'

'If he likes her,' said Ella, 'surely he would talk about her, wouldn't he?'

Jet shook his head. 'Nope. It's a guy thing. The more a guy likes a woman, the less inclined he is to talk about her with his friends.'

Ella laughed. 'What? So if he doesn't like her, he'll talk about her? If he likes her, he won't?'

'Yep. If a guy simply fancies a girl, he can make jokes, comment about how sexy she is and how much he'd like to get her into bed, stuff like that. But when he really likes her, he's more respectful. He'll still say how pretty she is, and how hot she looks, but not in the same way. He'll become more protective of her. He won't want his friends leering after her. Although he won't mind in the least if they're jealous. I'm not saying every guy behaves that way, but most of the guys I know, do. Bear was really torn up when Alexia dumped him to go out with me, but I was such a jerk back then I didn't even notice. It's only since … well since I met Mia, that I've realised a few things. And I'm pretty sure Bear would take Alexia back in a heartbeat.'

'Really?' Ella seemed quite excited. 'Then maybe we should try and get them together.'

'I wouldn't,' Jet said. 'Bear's a bit like me on that score. The more you push him in one direction, he'll force himself to go in the other.'

Mia laughed. 'Pig-headed and stubborn, you mean?' She grinned at Bree. 'You won't believe what I had to do to get this guy to start dating me.'

'But it was worth it, wasn't it?' Jet looked into Mia's eyes and smiled.

Mia nodded and smiled back. 'Absolutely.'

Ella tutted. 'God, you two. Get a room. But hold on, because this could get very complicated.

Bear fancies Alexia, but she's got the hots for Garrick, who is so messed up he might very well fall into bed with her, even though she's almost the spitting image of his dead girlfriend, and I really don't think would be his best choice. And then there's Bree.'

'What?' Again, Breanna almost choked.

Jet looked confused. 'What's Bree got to do with any of this?'

Ella grinned. 'That's the question we've been asking all morning.'

Breanna put her fork down and coughed. 'Thank you for a lovely lunch and for such a productive morning, but I think I need some air. I'm getting a bit of a headache. I hope you don't mind, but I'd quite like to go for a walk.' She got to her feet and threw Ella an icy stare.

'Of course.' Mia gave her an understanding smile. 'Ella has that effect on people.'

'Oh, it was only a joke,' Ella said. 'Don't go, Bree. I promise I'll shut up.'

Breanna forced a smile. 'I really do have a headache coming on. And I would like to get some air.' She picked up her plate to take it to the sink but Mia reached out a hand to stop her.

'Leave that.' She glared at Ella. 'I'll get Ella to clear up. You go, Bree. And enjoy your walk. We'll pick you up this evening around seven-thirty. Is that okay?'

Breanna nodded. 'That sounds perfect.'

Jet grinned. 'And by then, we'll have found some parcel tape to stick over Ella's mouth.'

Mia showed Breanna to the door. 'She doesn't mean any harm, Bree. She simply doesn't think sometimes. And if anything Mum or I said earlier offended you in any way, I apologise for both of us. Sometimes we forget we're all grown women and behave like fourteen-year-olds.'

'It's okay. I'm not offended. I'm just a bit embarrassed.' Mia handed her her coat and she shrugged it on with a sigh. 'The truth is, Mia, I've had a crush on Garrick Swann since we were six. And I know I haven't seen him for years, but last night, when he turned up at the cottage...' She raised her arms in the air and shook her head '...I can't explain it, but I felt exactly the same as I did the last time I saw him over seventeen years ago. And I know it's stupid. I know he's not interested in me and never will be. But, I suppose I'm a bit like Jet's friend, Bear. The heart wants what the heart wants.'

'I had no idea you felt that way about Garrick.' Mia was clearly surprised. 'Not all those years ago. Not when you were seventeen. Although to be honest, I'd also had a crush on him for years, so that's probably why I didn't notice. I was too wrapped up in my own feelings. I even dyed my hair red once, in the hope it might make him like me as more than a friend. It didn't.'

'He did kiss you once though,' Breanna said. 'It was on your sixth birthday. I remember because

I was rather jealous. I'd kissed him myself on my sixth birthday, several months before, but he turned and ran away from me.' She laughed, even though it wasn't funny as far as she was concerned. Not then, Not now.

'Did he? Oh yes. I remember. Ella teased him about it for a long time afterwards.'

Breanna nodded. 'Yes. For years.'

Mia took Breanna's hands in hers and smiled.

'Anyway. You know what? Things change. Garrick did like me last year. He liked me a lot. What I'm saying is, you never know, Bree. Love can take us all by surprise. Look at me and Jet. There's always hope.'

Breanna smiled back. 'I suppose so. But I don't expect anything to come of it. I only told you because you've been so unbelievably brilliant to me, and I don't want to hide anything from you. But miracles do happen. Meeting you again and all this happening is pretty miraculous. Perhaps it's not too far-fetched to think it's possible for Garrick to be interested in me. Although perhaps we only get one miracle in a lifetime.'

Mia laughed. 'I don't know about that. I got several in less than a year. Discovering I had a great-aunt Mattie. Moving down here. Inheriting her fortune. Meeting Jet. Falling in love. Him asking me to marry him. And believe me, before I was told about Mattie's will last March, and moved down here in May, my future was looking pretty boring.'

'Wow. I'll keep my fingers crossed then.'

'I'll keep mine crossed too. And I'll tell you another thing. And I said this to Jet not so long ago. There's something about Little Pondale that's almost magical. Everyone who comes here seems to find happiness or love. Sometimes both. Hettie Turner will tell you all sorts of superstitions about this place. Not to go to Frog's Hollow on a Monday because that's bad. But going skinny-dipping there on Midsummer's Eve may help you find your true love. Then there's the cave at Rainbow's End. And I have to say, that does seem to be spookily accurate. You say the name of the person you love and if it comes back as an echo, they'll be yours. But I think that may only be at Halloween. I'll have to check with Hettie. Then, of course, there's the Wishing Tree. But that's December, so that's too long to wait. Anyway. What I'm saying is, this place is special. If you want something enough, there's a very good chance you may get it.'

'Wow. I can't wait to meet Hettie Turner and hear all about it.'

'Hmm. You may regret saying that once you've met her. No. That's mean of me. Hettie's lovely and she's helped us all in lots of ways. I'll see you tonight. Enjoy your walk. Oh. But I do agree with one thing Ella said. You don't want to be Garrick's rebound girl, Bree. You want to be the one he falls in love with.'

Chapter Fifteen

Would an alien from a far-off planet, landing his spaceship on the village green cause more of a stir in Little Pondale?

The moment Breanna set foot on Lily Pond Lane, after crossing over from Seaside Road, curtains twitched in the chocolate-box cottages and heads popped up from behind hedges, all eyes studying 'the stranger in their midst'. But one or two people who were outside, tidying their gardens did at least wish her a good afternoon. She smiled and returned their greetings, admiring how neat and pretty all the gardens were and how twee the village was. It must have looked magical at Christmas, especially with all the snow. Children building snowmen, the quaint little pond to her left, no doubt covered with ice. Breanna loved Christmas. It would be wonderful to spend it in a place like this.

From out of nowhere, a young girl appeared beside Breanna. She was probably six or seven and wore a smart red coat. Her hair was the colour of melted toffee and she looked up at Breanna with big blue eyes and a friendly smile on her cupid's bow lips.

'Hello. My name's Daisy. What's yours?'

Breanna stopped and bent down to her level. 'Hello, Daisy. I'm Breanna. But everyone calls me Bree.'

The eyes grew even wider. 'Like the cheese? My mummy loves that cheese. I don't like it. But I do like sticking my fingers in it. It's all runny in the middle and feels like my model clay outside.' She giggled and clamped two small hands over her mouth. 'Oh. But I'm not supposed to do that.'

'It'll be our little secret.'

'Daisy?' A woman's voice called out from close by and a taller, older version of Daisy appeared from the driveway of one of the cottages. 'There you are. You know you shouldn't run off.'

'Sorry, Mummy. I came to say hello to the pretty lady.'

'Well next time, wait for me. Hi.' The woman smiled at Breanna. 'I'm Cathy, Daisy's mum. I hope she's not bothering you. You must be Bree. Mia and Ella's friend. And Mia's wedding planner, I believe.'

Cathy sounded as friendly and welcoming as her daughter. Breanna smiled, nodded and straightened up. 'Correct on all counts. Daisy's not bothering me at all. She gave me a wonderful welcome. It's lovely to meet you both.'

Daisy gave Breanna's coat a little tug. 'We're going to Jenny's to get cakes for tea. Jenny makes the bestest cakes.'

She pointed across the village green, beyond the pond to another quaint thatched cottage with a small shop window on one side, above which a sign announcing 'Lake's Bakes' swung gently in the afternoon breeze.

'Jenny makes the best cakes, sweetheart,' Cathy corrected.

Daisy gave a little frown. 'I know. I said she did.'

Cathy raised one brow and grinned at Breanna. 'Have you settled in? I haven't seen Willow Cottage, but I hear your nearest neighbour is a field away. If you ever want some company and Mia and Ella aren't around, my friend Christy and I live in Corner Cottage.'

'Thank you. That's kind of you. I only moved in yesterday and I need to sort out a few more things before I'm really settled, but Mia and Jet have been so generous and thoughtful, and it already feels like home. It'll take a while for me to get used to living in the middle of nowhere though. Have you lived here long?'

'No.' Cathy's laugh was melodic. 'You won't believe this but Christy and I brought Daisy, and Christy's daughter, Dylan here for Christmas. We only rented Corner Cottage for two weeks, but I met Leo, who was also in the village for the holidays. It was love at first sight, and here we are, still living in Corner Cottage. Christy now works in The Frog and Lily and is dating Toby Bywater, the owners' son, but I'm usually at home. Leo lives with us at the weekend, but during the week he still lives and works in London.'

'Wow. That was a whirlwind romance. Mia said this place was magical, and it sounds as if it definitely was for you and Leo. And for Christy if she's dating someone in the village too.'

Cathy nodded. 'There's definitely something special about this place. None of us ever want to live anywhere else now. Are you seeing anyone? Sorry. Don't answer that if you don't want to.'

'It's fine. No. I don't have a boyfriend at the moment. I'm a bit of walking disaster where romance is concerned. In fact, I'm a bit of a walking disaster, full stop. Accident-prone, my mum calls it.'

'Ah. Well, you never know. Perhaps you'll meet the man of your dreams in Little Pondale. I hope you do. But I'd better go. I told Leo I was only popping out for a couple of minutes to get some cakes. He's trying to fix Daisy's doll's house. She broke the front off its hinges earlier.'

'I didn't, Mummy. Dylan did.'

'Sorry. Dylan did.' Cathy playfully scrunched up Daisy's hair, and they both laughed before Cathy returned her attention to Breanna and whispered: 'I love Leo to bits, and he's one of the most intelligent men I've ever met, but DIY is not his forte, so Daisy and I nipped out in case the air turned blue.'

Breanna laughed. 'He should speak to Garrick. He was always good with his hands and could fix anything. And he has his own business making furniture now, so a doll's house should be a doddle for him to fix.'

'Of course. Why didn't I think of that? Thank you, Bree. You've just saved my weekend. I'll pop in and see if Garrick's free.'

'But the cakes, Mummy!' Daisy's face was a picture. She looked almost terrified as her big eyes darted a look first to Cathy and then fixed longingly in the direction of the bakery.

'We'll still get the cakes, sweetheart. We'll just call into Sunbeam Cottage first.'

'But…' Daisy let her voice trail off, pouted her lips, folded her arms across her body in an angry stance and let her chin drop to her chest as she heaved a large, discontented sigh.

'Anyone would think the world had ended,' Cathy said, rolling her eyes. 'Are you heading in this direction?' She pointed up the lane.

'Er. Yes. I was just going for a walk. I didn't have a particular destination in mind. I thought I'd take a look at the village.'

Cathy waved her arms outwards, a beaming smile on her face. 'Well, this is pretty much it. What you see is what you get. The bakery, the vets, the church and the pub, and a couple of lanes with cottages. Oh, and Frog Hill, of course, if you're into walking. And the beach. That's also a good place to walk. Especially at this time of year when the sea and the sky can be pretty dramatic. Although I suppose it could be dramatic at any time of year. As I've only been here since December, I don't really know.'

'Frog Hill is bigger than I expected. I wouldn't want to walk to the top of that just to get mobile phone reception.'

Cathy pointed towards the church. 'You can climb the three hundred steps of the steeple. But that's just as bad. Don't you have a landline at Willow Cottage?'

'Yes. I was merely remembering something Mia told me.'

Breanna smiled and fell into step beside Cathy and Daisy, the latter still sulking.

'Don't let Garrick see that expression on your face,' Cathy told Daisy. 'He won't let you see Flora if you've got a face like a sad sausage.'

Daisy instantly perked up. 'Can I play with her?'

Cathy shook her head. 'She's still too little for you to play with, sweetheart, but I'm sure you can say hello.'

With that, Daisy ran ahead, disappeared up a path and reappeared at the door of a bright yellow cottage, larger than most of the cottages in the lane. By the time Cathy and Breanna had caught up with her, the cottage door had opened and Garrick stood in the doorway, looking even more handsome in the daylight with sunshine dappled on his sandy hair.

Breanna's breath caught in her throat but she managed a few words. 'It was lovely chatting to you, Cathy. Goodbye Daisy. Hello Garrick.' She waved as Cathy said goodbye, and turned to continue on her way.

'Bree?' It was Garrick's voice. 'Hello. Won't you come in?'

'Er. I don't want to be in the way.' That was a stupid thing to say.

Garrick looked perplexed. 'Why would you be in the way? Please. Come in. If only for a second. Daisy here tells me she's got to say hello to Flora. Perhaps you'd like to do the same? Unless you're in a hurry.'

Cathy winked at her and smiled. 'You're not in a hurry, are you, Bree?'

'No. No I'm not. Er. Thanks, Garrick. I'd love to meet Flora.'

What else could she say? She could hardly tell him that being near him took her breath away. That it made her heart beat wildly and her head spin. That even after all these years, the best kiss she had ever experienced, the one kiss she still remembered, was just a split second as a six-year-old.

'Great.' Garrick sounded genuinely pleased.

'I hope we're not interrupting,' Cathy said, as she and Breanna stepped into the hall. 'Daisy. I mean, Dylan snapped the front off Daisy's doll's house and Leo's attempting to fix it, but it's not looking promising. Bree mentioned you, so I thought I'd come and ask if you would do me a huge favour and give Leo a hand. But only if you have the time. If not, that's absolutely fine. We'll pay of course.'

Garrick glanced at Bree, gave her an odd look, then turned his attention back to Cathy and smiled. 'That's no problem at all. Do you want to bring it here, or would you rather I came to you? I don't mind either way, but I'll have to bring Flora because Ella's still at Mia's, and Gill's busy writing, so I'd rather not disturb him. But as for paying me, forget it. I know we haven't known each other long, but I hope we're friends. It'll only take a few minutes and I'm not charging a friend for that.'

Cathy smiled. 'Thanks so much. If you ever need a babysitter, give me a shout, and I'll be happy to return the favour. But please don't tell Leo it'll only take a few minutes. He's been at it for at least twenty already. Daisy and I had to use the excuse of going to get some cakes just so that we could get out of the way.' She shook her head and laughed.

Garrick grinned. 'I'll tell you what. Buy me a cake and make me a cup of tea and I'll pretend it's a difficult job even for me and spend at least half an hour on it. Deal?'

'Absolutely. For half an hour you can have two cakes.'

Garrick laughed and patted his perfect stomach. 'I think I'd better stick to one, but thanks.' He gave Breanna a quick glance before smiling at Daisy. 'D'you want to say hello to Flora then, Little Princess?'

Daisy nodded excitedly. 'I won't play with her because she's too tiny. I'll just look. And maybe stroke her hair like this.' She ran the flat of her hand from the top of her head to her shoulder. 'Like Mummy does to me.'

Garrick's smile made Breanna's knees tremble and when he bent down and swept Daisy up in his arms, Breanna had to clamp a hand across her mouth to stop the loud sigh escaping.

What wouldn't she give to be Daisy right now?

She managed to follow them into the sitting room where Flora, clad in a pretty pink floral baby grow, was lying on a beautiful, quilted baby blanket in the middle of the floor, gurgling. Her little arms and legs were waving and kicking wildly like a puppet whose strings were all being pulled at once.

Garrick set Daisy down on the floor beside the blanket. After looking up at Cathy, Daisy reached out and stroked Flora's head, the tufts of pale red hair obviously tickling her fingers, because Daisy laughed and scratched her hand before repeating the process.

'If you'll keep an eye on Flora,' Garrick said to Cathy, 'I'll get my tools.'

'Of course.' Cathy walked towards the baby and sat on the floor beside Daisy, smiling at both children.

'You okay?' Garrick gave Breanna an odd look.

'What? Oh yes. I'm fine.'

'She won't bite. And she doesn't have any contagious diseases.' He was frowning and he sounded disappointed.

Breanna sighed and shook her head. 'No. But she might break.'

'Oh.' His sigh was of relief. 'That's what you're worried about?'

She looked him in the eye. 'Better to be safe than sorry. Disaster's my middle name.'

'Is it? I thought it was Madeleine, after your mother.' He grinned at her.

She sucked in a breath. 'You remembered?'

The grin grew wider. 'How could I forget? That's not all I remember. And you definitely used to be more daring. At least you were when you were six.'

Now she gasped. 'You remember that too? Oh my God. I'm so embarrassed.' The red heat fired up her cheeks as if Garrick had lit a match.

He was laughing, but in a warm and friendly way. 'They say you never forget your first kiss.'

'Your first?' It was certainly her first; she hadn't realised it was also his. 'Hmm. Especially if it's so bad you have to run away and you think you may be sick.'

He shook his head and an expression of remorse swept across his face as he frowned. 'I don't know why I did that.' He shrugged his shoulders. 'I was a six-year-old boy. That's the only excuse I have. And you took me by complete surprise.'

'You told me you only liked girls with red hair. That hasn't changed.' She bit her lip. Why on earth had she said that?

He was obviously thinking the same if the look on his face was anything to go by. 'Did I? That bit I don't remember. But again, I was six. And obviously an idiot.' Something flickered across his hazel eyes. 'I'm not six now. And I hope, no longer an idiot. Although actually that's not true. Lots of people will tell you I'm still behaving like an idiot. I'd better get my tools.' He turned away without another word.

Cathy gave a little cough and smiled when Breanna looked at her, craning her neck to look out into the hall as if checking that Garrick was out of earshot. 'Garrick? So that's the way the wind blows, is it?'

'What?' Breanna glanced over her shoulder, but thankfully Garrick was nowhere in sight. 'No. We're merely old friends.'

Cathy grinned and tapped her nose with her forefinger. 'Right you are. Merely friends. I'll remember that. Until I see the two of you arm in arm.'

Breanna tutted. 'You'll have a very long wait because that's never going to happen. Besides, he's dating Alexia.'

'Is he?' Cathy was still grinning. 'I wouldn't be so sure about that.'

'Oh?' Should she ask Cathy to elaborate? That would only confirm Cathy's suspicions. Better to let the matter drop. 'Flora's beautiful.'

'She is. Why don't you come closer?'

Breanna shook her head. 'I'm a danger, believe me.'

'Nonsense. But if you tell yourself that, you will be. Come on.'

Cathy jumped to her feet, reached out a hand and Breanna took it, allowing herself to be led towards the baby. They both sat down and Cathy indicated Breanna should sit cross legged. Cathy then gently lifted Flora from the blanket, cradling the baby's head and body against her as she carefully deposited the precious bundle in Breanna's arms.

'There,' said Cathy, smiling triumphantly. 'You're a natural.'

'I don't feel a natural.'

But as Breanna looked into Flora's eyes and saw part of Garrick reflected there, she relaxed, and a calmness swept over her like nothing she had ever felt before. But it was more than a mere feeling. It was an instinct. Almost a base need to care for and protect this child. She had read and heard that all mothers experienced this feeling for their children. But this baby wasn't hers. And the chances of her ever having one of her own were so remote that she'd pushed that thought into a box at the very back of her mind, closed the lid, padlocked it and cloaked it with an invisibility spell so that she wouldn't wake up in the middle of the night, longing for something she could never have. But here. Right now. In this split second, Breanna knew she could love this baby; this gurgling, giggling, treasure. This exceptional gift from the gods. A gift she would never receive for herself.

She didn't even hear Garrick come back. It was only when Daisy asked if they could go and get the cakes now, that Breanna realised there were others in the room besides just her and Flora.

As if awaking from a trance, she met Garrick's eyes, and there was something in the way he was watching her that she couldn't quite fathom. But as their gaze held, something else appeared there. A look she did understand. It was fear.

So in spite of what he had said, he was frightened at the thought of his child being in Breanna's arms.

Immediately, she placed the baby back onto the blanket and as she did so, Flora shrieked at the top of her lungs.

'Oh no! What've I done? Did I hurt her? I didn't mean to.'

She cast terrified eyes to Garrick then Cathy then back to Garrick who simply walked over and swept Flora up in his arms.

'She's fine. She merely wants to be held.'

Breanna clasped a hand to her chest. 'Thank heavens. I really thought I'd done something wrong.'

Cathy gave her a big hug and helped her to her feet. 'You were perfect. I told you. You're a natural.'

From the look on Garrick's face, that wasn't what he was thinking.

Breanna coughed lightly. 'Well. I think that's enough excitement for one day. I must go.'

'You're not coming with us?'

Garrick almost sounded disappointed. Or was that relief in his voice?

Breanna shook her head. 'No. I was on my way to church.'

'Church?'

'To look around. It looks pretty from the outside. And then I want to walk a little way up Frog Hill, and back along the beach, then home before it gets dark. And I've got to get ready for tonight.'

'Oh? Are you going somewhere special?'

Breanna met his eyes. As if he cared.

'To the pub with Mia and Jet. They're going to introduce me to everyone in the village. Well, anyone who's in the pub tonight, that is.'

'You know I said I'd repay the favour?' Cathy said to Garrick as Breanna was about to leave. 'Leo and I are having a quiet night in. I'm happy to babysit tonight.'

'Er.' Garrick seemed unsure what to do or say. 'Thanks, Cathy. But I was planning a quiet night in myself. Bye Bree. Enjoy your walk.' He cast Breanna a fleeting glance and stepped aside to let her pass.

'Bye Garrick. Bye-bye Flora. Lovely to meet you. And you, Cathy and Daisy.' Breanna walked to the door, her head held high, but as she was about to step outside she heard Cathy's voice.

'If you change your mind, Garrick. Just give me a shout.'

'Thanks,' he said. 'But I won't change my mind. Let's go and fix this doll's house.'

Breanna didn't wait. She hurried down the path, turned up the lane towards the church, and fought the urge to glance back over her shoulder.

Chapter Sixteen

It was four weeks before Breanna saw Garrick again. Four. Whole. Weeks.

It wasn't for want of trying on her part; she was beginning to think that Garrick was going out of his way to avoid her. She went over and over in her mind that day in Sunbeam Cottage. Had she done something to upset him? Had she said something? She had no idea what the problem was.

Equally worrying was the fact that neither Mia or Ella, or even Lori for that matter, seemed to want to discuss Garrick with her either. Each time she mentioned his name, casually of course, they gave each other odd looks and quickly changed the subject.

Thankfully, Breanna had other things to think about. Things that should have been far more important. Like Mia's wedding, for example. But Breanna couldn't stop her mind from wandering in Garrick's direction, no matter how hard she tried. Luckily for her, she was able to stop her feet from wandering towards his door.

And just because she hadn't seen him whilst Mia, Ella and Lori were loath to discuss him, it didn't mean Breanna had no news about him. On the contrary, it seemed that everyone else in the village was more than happy to tell Breanna how wonderful it was to see Garrick with a smile on his face. To see Garrick out pushing Flora's pram with Alexia by his side. To see Garrick in the pub … with Alexia. To see Garrick and Alexia going to rugby together, along with Gill, but Gill was clearly the gooseberry in that scenario.

There was an upside to this. Since that Saturday, four weeks ago, when Breanna had gone to the pub with Mia and Jet, and been introduced to everyone, the villagers had welcomed her with open arms and accepted her as a local. Well, almost. She had been told by more than one person that she wouldn't really be considered a *local* until she had lived in Little Pondale for at least twenty years. One of those people was Hettie Turner.

But even so, Hettie had kindly filled her in on all the comings and goings in the village and told her all the myths, mysteries, legends and superstitions. Hettie had even asked her husband, Fred to print them all out, along with all the do's and don'ts, like never going to Frog's Hollow on a Monday, unless you wanted to be thrown twenty feet in the air and land on your head on the bonnet of a car as her first husband, Hector had done.

Breanna had met Christy's boyfriend, Toby Bywater who was Alexia's brother. She had met

Toby and Alexia's dad, Alec who was recovering well since having a heart attack in January. He was even helping out behind the bar under the ever watchful eye of his wife, Freda, who had also given Breanna a very warm welcome.

She had also been asked out. Much to her surprise. By Rupert Day, the local vet and Jet's good friend. He'd told her to call him Bear.

'Everyone calls me Bear,' he said, leaning closer across the table in the pub on that first Saturday night. 'But not everyone gets to see me bare.' He had winked at her and nudged her arm. 'I think we're probably the only two single people in the village. D'you fancy getting naked?'

Spitting her mouthful of wine all over him was probably not the reaction he was expecting, but if you're going to say things like that to a virtual stranger, you must be prepared to accept the consequences.

She had apologised. She had even thanked him for his ... kind offer.

'I may live to regret this,' she said, having managed to recover from the surprise. 'But I think I'll have to say no. But thank you. It was lovely of you to offer. I need to concentrate on organising Mia's wedding though and getting the business off the ground. I don't really have time for a relationship.'

'Who said anything about a relationship?' His tone wasn't quite as seductive as he wiped himself down. 'I'm just talking about having a bit of fun.'

'Thank you. But I don't really think I'll have much time for fun, either.'

He looked her up and down and shrugged. 'Okay. No harm in asking. If you ever change your mind, or need a vet, or if you're ill and need a first responder, you know where to find me. Now let me get you another drink because I'm wearing your last one.' With that he had got up and smiled as if nothing at all odd had happened between them.

'So I see you've met Bear,' said Ella, who had been sitting close by throughout and was grinning from ear to ear.

'I see what you mean about him being a bit OTT. But he seems pretty harmless. And in a way, quite nice. He's definitely good-looking.'

'Whoa!' Ella said. 'Don't forget what Jet told us over lunch.'

'I haven't. But isn't Alexia keen on Garrick?'

Ella had shrugged. 'Yeah. But it doesn't mean Garrick's keen on her.'

Well, that was clearly wrong because since then, from everything Breanna had heard, Garrick seemed very keen on Alexia. Very keen indeed. Not that Ella would discuss the subject now.

And Breanna had plenty of things to keep her busy during those four weeks. As she expected, when her friend, Delphinie met Mia, they got on like a house on fire. Delphinie liked Ella's sketch, but they still flicked through some magazines and scanned the internet so that Delphinie had it clear in her mind exactly what Mia would and wouldn't like. No puffs, no huge bows, no candy floss petticoats, nothing too ostentatious. Simple, elegant with a hint of romance and perhaps a little sparkle here and there. Or maybe a fair amount of sparkle. Delphinie told Mia not to worry about a thing. She'd throw some ideas together and send the sketches to both Mia and Breanna. One week later, the design was agreed; Mia was over the moon and Breanna breathed a sigh of relief and ticked another thing off her list.

The bridesmaids' dresses were purchased 'off the peg' from a bridal shop in London. Not the one in which Breanna and Mia had met. The dresses were pale pink, off the shoulder, full-length, shimmering satin, tight fitting from the bodice to just above the knee where folded pleats of pale blue fanned out each side. As Ella and Jet's half-sister, Tiffany both had blonde hair, the pale pink suited them perfectly, and neither dress would require much alteration, but Delphinie was happy to oblige. Pale pink satin court shoes were found to match, and Mia bought shoes which were almost a perfect match to her own dress design.

Another friend of Breanna's, this one working as a freelance hair and make-up artist, was booked for the wedding day and confirmed she would be happy to come a couple of days before and stay at Little Pond Farm to try out various hairstyles and make-up.

'Who knew,' Ella said, as things progressed, 'that you had so many useful contacts, Bree?'

'I'm as surprised as you. I've known them all for years, and was always aware what they did for a living, but I never connected the dots. It took Mia's offer, and her faith in me to make me see what was right in front of me.'

'Life's odd like that,' said Ella. 'Sometimes we can't see what's right in front of our noses.'

'Love's often like that too,' added Lori. 'We can see someone every day without realising that they're the perfect person to share our lives with. Then suddenly something happens and wham. We realise we're in love and wonder why it took us so long to see it.'

'But sometimes,' said Breanna, 'one of us knows we're in love with the other, but the other's not in love with us.'

Which was exactly how things were with her and Garrick. Except she hadn't seen him every day. She hadn't seen him for four whole weeks.

Breanna pushed open the door of Lake's Bakes and the little bell tinkled overhead.

'Hello, Bree,' Jenny Lake said, smiling warmly. 'Isn't it wonderful weather? Perfect for Mother's Day weekend. And so warm. It's usually draughty in this bakery every time the door opens, but today all I'm wearing is this T-shirt. I don't feel cold at all. Not just a T-shirt.' She lifted her leg high enough for Bree to see her jeans behind the counter. 'I'm also wearing jeans.' Jenny laughed and tugged the scrunchie band on her wild red hair a little tighter. 'What can I offer you today?'

Breanna laughed jovially. She liked Jenny a lot. And Jenny's boyfriend Glen, who was the vicar of St Michael and All Angels. She'd met them in the pub on that first Saturday night and since then had seen them several times, including every Tuesday at choir practice, which Mia, Jet, Ella and Gill also attended. Apparently, Garrick and Alexia used to go last summer, but they had obviously found a better way to entertain themselves on Tuesday nights. For the last four weeks at least.

'I'd like some cakes, please. And some bread. And an extra-scrumptious cake for Mother's Day. My mum's coming down to stay this weekend. I'm picking her up from the station on the early evening train tonight. I haven't seen her since I went back up two weeks ago to help her move, and I really want the weekend to be special. Mia and Jet have invited us to dinner tomorrow night, and on Sunday I'm taking Mum to the pub for lunch.'

'I'm sure she'll have a lovely time. Just being able to spend the weekend with you will make it special.'

'I hope so. Are you doing anything?'

'No. My parents aren't around and neither are Glen's, so it'll just be us. Although he'll be busy at the church for a lot of it. But we'll get to spend plenty of time together. It's a shame you don't have someone special in your life. Other than your mum, obviously. No news on that front?'

'No. Not that I'd have time for a relationship. Setting up *The Wright Wedding*, getting all the business cards and everything done, along with organising Mia's wedding is taking up all of my time. Not that I'm complaining. I love every minute of it. Especially since having my lovely new car for the last three and a half weeks. It's so wonderful to just jump in the car and go and meet florists, printers, and photographers and so on. And thank you so much for mentioning my business to anyone and everyone who comes in here. I've had loads of enquiries. At this rate, Mia says that maybe I should think of taking on someone part-time to help me. She and Jet are so incredible. They've said it's entirely up to me what I do and how I run it, but that if I need any additional funds on top of what they're already given me, I mustn't be afraid to ask. Honestly, Jenny. I still have to pinch myself sometimes to believe this is all happening.'

'I know. They're both unbelievably generous and genuinely lovely people. I understand that all the RSVPs for the wedding are back and everyone has said yes, and how much they loved the seeds with the invitations. Not that I'm surprised. That was such a lovely idea.' She crossed her hands over her heart. 'Oooh. And the photo of Mia standing slightly in front of Jet, with his arms wrapped around her, and their heads turned so that they were looking into each other's eyes, actually brought tears to my eyes. It was so beautiful and romantic.'

Breanna nodded enthusiastically. 'To mine too. They're simply the perfect couple. And anyone can see how much they love one another. It must be wonderful to have someone who loves you as much as Jet loves Mia. But you have that of course, with Glen.'

Jenny sighed dramatically and fluttered her eyelashes for added effect. 'Yes. I think I do. I'm a very lucky girl. And you'll find love one day, Bree. Trust me. You will. So, how's it all going with the wedding? I can't wait to get started on the cake.'

'It's going really well. So far. And I haven't even had any disasters. Well, not many. Perhaps having all those white doves flying into the air after being released from those large white cardboard hearts, and the birds all flapping about in a confined space over everyone's heads at choir practice the other day, wasn't my best idea. But Hettie did tell us all that having bird poo land on us was an omen of good luck. So virtually everyone, including you and Glen, should have a substantial amount of good luck coming their way.'

Breanna and Jenny both laughed.

'You've definitely decided against the doves, I take it?'

Breanna nodded. 'Against live ones, yes. But Mia told me about Jet's proposal, and the Wishing Tree and how beautiful he had made it look with all the lights, and with everyone's wishes hanging from ribbons, and that gave me an idea, which Mia loved, but wants to keep a secret from Jet until the day.'

Jenny leant forward. 'Ooh. That sounds exciting. Can you tell me? I promise I won't tell anyone.'

'I know you wouldn't. Mia did say that I could tell anyone I was sure wouldn't give the game away to Jet. And Jet's arranged a surprise for Mia, which she won't know until the day, but he won't mind you knowing that.' Breanna glanced around to check that no one else could hear despite her being the only person in the bakery with Jenny. 'So as you know, the reception's at The Frog and Lily, but there's going to be a huge marquee in the garden and lights all along the hedges and trees and even down to posts along the beach, where there'll be a large wooden dance floor beneath open skies. Assuming we have good weather. If not, a canopy will be erected overhead.'

'I like the sound of that. Dancing under the stars is so romantic.'

'Let's hope it doesn't rain. Anyway, Mia thinks Freda and Alec are doing the food. But they're not. Jet's friend, Luke Martindale and his business partner, the famous TV chef and Mia's favourite, Xavier Sombeanté are doing the catering for the entire event. There's going to be a surprise champagne breakfast at Little Pond Farm for Mia, Lori, the bridesmaids and everyone else involved in getting Mia ready for the wedding. And that, I'm glad to say, includes me. It also includes you, because you're making the cake. I'll give you times and details nearer the time.'

'Me? Oh gosh. How wonderful. A champagne breakfast. Wow. I'd better get Glen, or someone, to carry the cake to its position in the marquee then, just in case.' Jenny laughed and winked.

'Good idea. Then there's the wedding at two, followed by a five-course sit down meal in the marquee, cocktails and canapes between six-thirty and seven, and a late-night buffet for anyone who can last until the early hours of the following morning.'

'Oh good heavens! That sounds absolutely fantastic.'

'I know. Trying to fob Mia off about the menus though, is proving difficult, but Freda and Alec are in the know, so they've agreed to go along with everything as if they're doing the catering.'

'And Mia's surprise for Jet?'

'In the marquee and around the edges of the dance floor, there'll be massive, fake marble pots because the real ones are far too heavy, with silver birch trees, sprayed with fake snow, and hung with dangling crystals to look like ice and myriad white fairy lights. That's as close as we can get to a copy of the Wishing Tree because the real Wishing Tree is a rare, white oak, and I can't find any small ones of those. I've managed to find, through a friend I know who works in theatre stage design, several life-sized but imitation white doves. The feathers are real but the birds aren't, and their eyes are gemstones. It sounds a bit tacky but, believe me, they're beautiful. They'll be perched here and there on each tree. And, when the guests arrive at the church, everyone will be handed a white and silver card and a silver pen to write a note of good wishes to Mia and Jet. We've got someone to collect the cards and they'll be hung with white ribbon on each of the trees and retrieved afterwards for Mia and Jet to keep.'

'Oh how wonderful! It'll be beautiful, Bree.'

'I hope so. I think it will. God, I really hope it doesn't rain.'

Breanna was so engrossed that she nearly jumped out of her skin when the bell tinkled above the door, and Jenny seemed just as startled. But Breanna was more so when Garrick and Alexia stepped inside.

Chapter Seventeen

'Garrick!' Breanna blinked. 'And Alexia. Um. Hello.'

Garrick gave Breanna a fleeting glance and a perfunctory nod. Alexia was more cordial.

'Hello, Jenny. Hello, Bree. How are things going with the wedding planning?'

'Very well, thank you. How are you?'

'Fine, thanks. We've just popped in to get a cake for Garrick's mum.'

Jenny jumped in. 'Are your parents coming down for the weekend?'

Garrick shook his head. 'No. We're going up to see them.'

Breanna tried to stop the gasp escaping, but failed, then tried to turn it into a cough and couldn't stop.

'You okay, Bree?' Jenny asked. She grabbed a small bottle of water from the shelves behind her and tossed it across the counter to Breanna. 'Drink that. It's probably because we've been talking so much.'

Breanna gratefully twisted off the cap and a fountain of fizzy water sprayed over Garrick, who had moved closer to her, a concerned look on his face. The water splattered across the T-shirt that clung loosely to his broad chest. Mortified, Breanna wiped the droplets with her hand, her fingers tingling as they felt every ripple of the firm muscles beneath. The problem was, she was still holding the bottle, so even more water sloshed down Garrick's front.

'Bree!'

'Oh my God! I'm sorry.' She quickly put the half-empty bottle on the counter and hastily turned back to Garrick, now rubbing his chest with the palms of both hands.

Jenny's laughter reverberated in her ears. 'I think Garrick's okay now, Bree.'

'Yeah,' said Alexia. 'If you rub much harder you'll wear the material away.'

Garrick said nothing, but when Breanna realised what she was doing, and met his eyes, there was an odd look in them.

'Oh no. I'm sorry.' She rapidly backed away, stuffing her hands into the pockets of her jeans, and caught sight of the questioning look on Alexia's beautiful face.

'Thanks,' Garrick said, after what seemed like an eternity but was probably a matter of seconds. 'I needed cooling off.'

'I must go,' said Bree, dashing to the door and bashing Garrick's shoulder in her haste.

'First, you soak him,' Alexia said, but her laughter held no merriment. 'Now you're trying to beat him up. What's the poor guy done to you?'

'Nothing. Sorry. He's done nothing. Nothing at all. It's me. It's all my fault. Sorry. Bye.'

'Bree!' Jenny called after her. 'What about your bread and cakes?'

'I'll come back later. There's somewhere I need to be.' She raced out of the door to where her car was parked, got in, slammed the door and drove off as quickly as she could.

How could she be so stupid? She had stood there in front of Jenny and Alexia as good as stroking Garrick's chest and torso. Why hadn't he moved away? Why hadn't he stopped her? Why hadn't she stopped herself? She was really losing the plot. She had to get over this ridiculous crush on Garrick Swann. Especially now. If Garrick was taking Alexia up to London for the weekend that could only mean one thing. That Garrick and Alexia were officially a couple. A serious couple, if he was taking her to meet his parents and spend the weekend. Particularly as it was Mother's Day on Sunday.

Her heart thumped so hard that it echoed in her ears. Was she seeing stars? Was her vision blurring? Were her arms, fingers and legs really tingling?

She quickly did a three-point turn and drove back the way she had come, but this time continuing past Lake's Bakes and pulling up outside the vets. She parked haphazardly and raced inside. There was no sign of a receptionist, only an elderly man with an equally elderly dog of an indeterminable breed, both sitting patiently on neighbouring, plastic chairs.

'Is Bear free?' She clutched her chest.

'Bear. What bear? Where?' The old man looked around and so did his dog. 'There's no bear in here.'

'Bear! I need to see him urgently. Um. Rupert. Rupert Day. I think I may be having a heart attack.'

'You're in the wrong place. He's a vet, not a doctor.'

'What?'

Thankfully, Bear appeared from a door behind a screen.

'What's going on? Bree? What're you doing here?'

The old man piped up, shaking his head. 'Looking for a bear and a doctor.'

'I'm having a heart attack, I think,' said Bree, still clutching her chest.

'You'd better come in then. But I don't think you're having a heart attack by the looks of you. More like a panic attack. Mr Davies? Would you and Sergeant Major be kind enough to let my friend go before you? It'll only be a couple of minutes.'

'Right you are, Mr Day. The poor young lady obviously needs some help.' Then under his breath, but loud enough for Breanna to hear. 'But not from a vet, eh, Sergeant Major?'

He tapped his head with his finger and nodded at his dog who nodded back as Breanna stumbled past towards Bear's consulting room, mumbling a thank you to the man on the way, even though he clearly thought she was completely mad.

Chapter Eighteen

Damn Garrick, and to hell with Alexia. There was no way their relationship was going to ruin Breanna's weekend with her mum.

Well, certainly not the rest of the weekend. It had already put a dampener on Friday night. After discovering her suspected heart attack was indeed a panic attack, she had been ordered home to rest, fallen asleep and woken up in the nick of time to make it to the station to meet Madeleine's train. Thank goodness there were no speed cameras between Little Pondale and Big Whipping station. But she nearly had a second panic-cum-heart-attack when a rabbit shot out in front of her. She avoided it – and smashing her car into a hedge – by the merest whisker.

Having forgotten the bread and cakes, their supper had been only half of what Breanna had planned and when Madeleine asked if Breanna had seen much of Garrick, Breanna nearly bit her mum's head off.

'You're overworking and overtired,' Madeleine said. 'Let's have an early night. My bed looks very comfy.'

'I'm so sorry, Mum. I wanted this evening to be really special. I've just got a lot on my mind.'

'It has been special, darling.' Madeleine squeezed Breanna's hand. 'And it's lovely to see you're doing so well. This cottage is so welcoming and cosy and the little personal touches you've added make it feel like a home from home for me. Your new car is wonderful. I felt like royalty when I saw you waiting at the station. I can't wait to see Mia and Lori again, and Ella too. And the bridegroom to be, of course. I'm so proud of you, my darling. I knew your time would come. Now all you need to do is find yourself a young man and settle down. Then perhaps, I could stop worrying about you.'

'Oh, Mum. There's no need to worry about me. I'm happy as I am. Especially now. With all this.' Breanna waved her arms around her. 'But as it happens, I've got a date next week. Monday night, in fact.'

'So that's why you've been on edge all evening? And when were you going to tell me this? Never mind. Is he nice? Handsome? What does he do for a living?'

Breanna cleared her throat. 'He's handsome, certainly. And yes, I think he's nice. He's a vet, and lives in the village. And he's a first responder too. Oh, and he's friends with Jet, Mia's fiancé.'

'How wonderful, darling! A vet. My, my. You have done well for yourself.'

'It's just a date, Mum. I think we're the only two single people in the village.'

'Well, you hang onto him, my darling girl. Vets don't grow on trees, you know. Especially handsome vets. You need to get yourself a pet.'

'A pet? Why?'

'So you've got an excuse to pop in to see him every now and then.'

Breanna shook her head. 'I don't think me getting a pet is a very good idea. I'd probably lose it, knowing me.'

'A dog would be good. A big dog. Especially living way out here. I know you said it was a farm cottage in the middle of nowhere, but I didn't expect nowhere to be quite so, well, sparsely populated.'

Breanna laughed. 'Yes. That surprised me, too.'

'Right. I'm off to bed. Don't stay up too late, darling. You need your beauty sleep. Especially for your date with the vet on Monday.'

Saturday had gone much better. Breanna only thought of Garrick and Alexia a couple of times. Okay. A couple of hundred times. But less than she had on Friday night. She even got up early, drove to Lake's Bakes and bought some bread and the cakes she was after. For Mother's Day she chose a large cream and jam sponge cake, crammed full with raspberries, topped with pink icing and scattered with white and dark chocolate curls, and a small pile of raspberries in the centre. A selection of scones with cream and jam, apple turnovers, and Jenny's famous sticky buns for little treats today.

After breakfast, Breanna had taken her mum for a drive. They went to Rainbow's End, so that Madeleine could see the sea, then drove through the village and home for bread and soup for lunch and an afternoon nap for Madeleine.

Lori and Franklin picked them up and drove them to Mia and Jet's for dinner, giving Breanna time to dwell on what, exactly, Garrick and Alexia would be doing, whilst Lori and Madeleine made up for lost time and chatted about 'the old days'. Franklin sang quietly along to a softly playing compilation of his favourite singer, King of Country Music, George Strait.

Lori made the introductions when they arrived at Little Pond Farm and when Mia ushered them into the dining room, Breanna was surprised to see the table was laid for six.

'Aren't Ella and Gill joining us?'

'They've gone to London for the weekend.'

So it wasn't merely Garrick and Alexia and baby Flora; it was the entire family. A ripple of ice ran through Breanna as she had visions of Garrick proposing. But that was ridiculous, wasn't it? Surely he would wait? It had been less than three months since Fiona passed. Wasn't it a bit too quick to rush into marriage with someone else?

Even someone as beautiful and clearly wonderful, as Alexia.

Breanna had little appetite and half the conversations went over her head. She wasn't really listening. It was only when her mum told everyone, just as they finished dessert, how pleased she was that her daughter was dating a vet that Breanna was pulled unwillingly from her vision of an ecstatic Garrick and Alexia showing off the engagement ring.

'What?' Breanna said, as all eyes turned to her.

'You're dating Bear?' Jet seemed as surprised as Mia.

'Since when?' Mia asked, glancing at Jet.

'Who's Bear?' queried Madeleine.

'The vet,' said Lori.

'I thought the guy had a thing for Alexia,' added Franklin in his laid-back Texan drawl. 'But hell, what do I know?'

Breanna tutted. 'Alexia's spending the weekend with Garrick. So Bear's completely out of luck.'

Jet leant back in his chair. 'Well, not completely. If he's dating you, perhaps he's finally moving on. But I might have a quick word with him in any case.'

'Alexia's not with Garrick,' Mia said, staring at Breanna. 'He and Flora have gone to London with Ella and Gill to see their parents.'

'But Alexia's gone too.'

'No, she hasn't.'

'They were in the bakery on Friday buying a cake.'

'Would someone mind telling me,' said Madeleine, rather louder than was required, 'just what exactly is going on?'

Lori grabbed the wine bottle and began topping up their glasses. 'A complete misunderstanding by the sound of it.'

Chapter Nineteen

Breanna was ecstatic. Okay, Garrick and Alexia might be dating, but at least he hadn't taken her to London to meet his parents. He hadn't fallen head over heels in love. He wasn't planning to propose. Well, maybe he had and perhaps he was. Just because he hadn't taken Alexia with him didn't necessarily exclude the other options.

The ecstasy didn't last long. Even if he didn't love Alexia, it made no difference to Breanna's chances. He still wasn't interested in her. He'd made that abundantly clear.

But at least she wouldn't have to see a massive diamond sparkling on Alexia's finger, burning into Breanna's heart like a laser beam.

And Breanna did have her date with Bear to look forward to on Monday. She wasn't looking forward to it yet, but that was understandable, wasn't it? She was concentrating on ensuring her mum had a good weekend. And now that she knew Alexia hadn't gone to London, Breanna could really enjoy herself too.

By the time Breanna took Madeleine to the station at ten a.m. on Monday, they had been to church on Sunday morning, gone to Hettie and Fred's for coffee, had a delicious lunch of roast beef and all the trimmings, followed by date and butterscotch pudding at The Frog and Lily. Later, they invited Lori and Franklin for afternoon tea and spent a quiet Sunday evening, curled up in front of the fire on a suddenly chilly night, playing a game of Scrabble.

'I'll definitely come again,' Madeleine said, as she waved a tearful farewell on the station platform.

'You're welcome any time.'

'Good luck with your vet tonight. And I know I don't have to tell you this, because you're a sensible girl, but don't let him talk you into bed on your first date. He may be a vet and a very good catch, but no one buys the cow if they can get the milk for free.'

Breanna nodded. 'Thanks for that, Mum. I'll bear it in mind. No pun intended.'

'That's a very strange name for a man. Do you think it's because he's wild and rugged? Or because he hugs like a bear? Or because he's cuddly like a teddy bear?'

'None of the above. It's his middle name. His parents named him that because he was conceived on a bear watching holiday in Canada.'

'Oh I say. Well, have fun. It's a shame I didn't get to meet him. Send me a photo.'

'I'll do that, Mum.'

As much as Breanna loved her mum, was it wrong of her to breathe a sigh of relief when Madeleine finally boarded the train?

Breanna spent the day ticking more things off her list for Mia and Jet's wedding. It was now the 1st of April – not a date that boded well for doing business … or for Breanna's date with Bear that evening, so Breanna stayed at home and listened to wedding music on her laptop and searched for suppliers of confetti. She would contact them another time.

Relaxed, showered and dressed, she was ready by seven-thirty. Bear was picking her up at eight. Madeleine called at seven forty-five.

'Thanks again for the weekend. Enjoy yourself tonight. But don't forget what I said about the milk.'

'I won't, Mum.'

After several further words of advice, Madeleine rang off and Breanna waited, growing more anxious as the minutes ticked away.

Bear was handsome. He was nice. And yes, he was a vet. But if he was still in love with Alexia what was the point in dating him? What was the point even if he wasn't in love with Alexia? Bear wasn't the one for Breanna. Her heart and her head both told her that. Was she the type of girl who could just have fun? Probably. If Garrick wasn't around.

But Garrick was around. Okay, Breanna hadn't seen him much. And nothing would come of it if she did. But could she really sit in the pub and laugh and joke with Bear, knowing Garrick was merely doors away? Could she kiss Bear good night, knowing she would rather be kissing Garrick? She certainly wouldn't be giving any milk away. Metaphorically speaking or otherwise. How could she have sex with Bear, or any other man now, knowing that any minute she might say Garrick's name, or see his face?

God, she had it bad.

The ridiculous thing was, that even though she was sure that she and Garrick would never have any kind of relationship other than as friends, there was still that lingering hope. That tiny seed of doubt that kept sprouting into bloom whenever she saw him, or heard someone mention his name. That tiny flicker that burst into flame with a look, or a smile, or even a kind word. Not that there had been any of those things for weeks.

But on that first night, when he had come to Willow Cottage there had been something in the way he looked at her. Something in the way that torch beam had turned back in her direction. Had she imagined it? Was it simply wishful thinking?

When she was six she had been brave. She had taken a chance. A risk. And Garrick had run away. But hadn't he said that he had been an idiot? That he wouldn't run away now. What had he meant by that? Why hadn't she thought of this before? Why now? When she was waiting for another man to take her out.

The knock on the door startled her. Taking a deep breath she opened it and saw the smile on Bear's handsome face.

'Hello,' he said. 'You look lovely.'

'Hello, Bear. So do you. But I think we need to talk.'

Chapter Twenty

Mia was getting excited, and she wasn't the only one. Jet had taken to humming the Wedding March, Lori got tearful every time she looked at Mia, and Ella kept coming up with increasingly more ludicrous ideas for Mia's wedding.

'You could arrive in a hot air balloon. Ooh! And Jet could drop in by parachute, like James Bond.'

'Yes. And I'd be blown off course and end up in the sea, and Jet would land on top of one of the stone angels on the church roof.

'Better than one of the stone angels landing on top of him.'

Mia threw Ella one of her quelling looks. Not that it quelled Ella in the slightest.

'You could have trumpeters either side of the church doors playing the arrival of the Queen of Sheba, or whatever it's called. Lots of people have that at weddings.'

'I'm having Johann Pachelbel's, Canon in D Major, played on violins.'

'You could have one of those ice hotel bar thingies made on the beach.'

'It'll be May, and hopefully very warm. Ice would melt. Besides, we've already decided on the reception and the marquee. The only thing I'm slightly concerned about is whether the Bywaters can really handle the catering. I know Freda said they could and Toby told me they'd hire lots of extra staff, but still.'

'I'll be keeping a close eye on all that,' Breanna said, 'Don't you worry about a thing. The catering will be brilliant. Far, far better than you can imagine.'

'Really? Because I'm having second thoughts about the menu. It's a bit boring, isn't it? Perhaps we should have a rethink.'

'No!' Breanna shrieked. 'Believe me, Mia. You definitely don't need to rethink the catering.'

'That's what Jet says. But I'm not so sure.'

'Please, Mia. Leave that with me. I'll sort it all out with the Bywaters. Now, confetti. Yes or no? Rice or paper? Or are you thinking real flower petals?'

Ella almost spilt the coffee she was pouring as she refilled Mia's mug. 'Oh! What about having white feathers? You know. Now that you're not having real doves.'

'No, Ella.' Mia and Breanna agreed.

'Chocolate coins in silver wrappings? The kids at the wedding would love that. So would the adults like me.' Ella had a huge grin on her face.

'Handfuls of chocolate coins being thrown at me and Jet? Hmm. What a good thing you're an editor and not a wedding planner.' Mia laughed and gave Ella a friendly shove.

Breanna shuddered dramatically. 'And all those sticky, chocolate covered fingers brushing against the bridal gown and all the ladies' finery. Having kids at a wedding is a big enough potential disaster. Chocolate would make it a certainty.'

'I'd like it to be biodegradable, whatever confetti we have. And someone needs to hand out small boxes of it to everyone as they enter the church. Craig says wedding photos with lots of confetti in the air are always popular. And is it possible to get pink, blue and white confetti, d'you think? To go with the wedding theme colours.'

'I'll see what I can do. Right. I think that's everything.' Breanna smiled triumphantly. 'Now it's just a matter of chasing things up and making sure it all goes smoothly on the day.'

'Thank you, thank you, thank you. I can't believe it's all going so well. I don't mean I'm surprised you've done it, Bree. I mean I'm surprised you've done it all so easily and quickly and taken all the headache and worry away from me. I'm so glad we bumped into you that day in London. I know Mum and Ella are brilliant, but the three of us would never have been able to pull this off. You're a natural, Bree. An absolute genius. And I'm going to tell everyone and anyone. Oh no!

What's wrong? Was it something I said? I meant it as a compliment.'

Breanna wiped her eyes and shook her head. 'I know you did. I'm sorry. I'm feeling a little over emotional, I think. It's just when you called me a natural, it … it reminded me of something else. Something Cathy said a few weeks ago.' She sniffed, grabbed a tissue and blew her nose. 'Sorry.'

Mia glanced at Ella. 'That's okay. There's nothing to apologise for. I just hope I haven't upset you.'

'No, no. I'm fine.' She blew her nose again. 'Right then. I'd better chase the wine merchants. The one thing we don't want to do is run out of champagne on your Big Day.'

'Talking of Big Days,' Ella said, grinning. 'How did your date with Bear go last night? I tried to persuade Mia to come to the pub so that we could keep an eye on you, but she told me to grow up.' Ella stuck her tongue out at Mia and they both laughed.

'Yes, Bree. I'm sorry I didn't ask. Jet told me not to.'

Breanna gave an odd little grin. 'It went well, thanks. Very well indeed. Much better than expected actually.'

'It did?' Mia and Ella exchanged glances.

'Yes.' Breanna's grin grew wider. 'It did. In fact, we're seeing each other again on Friday.'

Chapter Twenty-One

It had been a hectic couple of weeks for Breanna. Mia's wedding was under control but thanks to Mia, and to Jenny, and all the contacts and suppliers Breanna had been making, *The Wright Wedding* was now being inundated with requests for Breanna's wedding-planning services.

On top of that, she had thrown herself enthusiastically into village life. Choir practice on Tuesday, jogging with Mia, Ella and Lori along the beach most mornings, baking, also with Mia, Ella and Lori on Wednesdays, the pub quiz on Fridays, and, of course, fitting in as many dates as possible with Bear.

She smiled to herself as she finished typing an email to Delphinie confirming a date for Mia to have her first fitting for her wedding dress. She straightened her back, stretched out her arms, and yawned. She would go to bed the minute she was sure the email had gone through. She hadn't had anywhere near as much to drink tonight as Mia and

Ella had, but she was definitely feeling sleepy. Perhaps she had been overdoing it?

Everyone in the village thought she was definitely overdoing something. If only they knew the truth about her and Bear. What would they say? Would they be annoyed? Would they feel misled? Was the scheme she and Bear had concocted even working? She did feel bad about keeping the truth from Mia and Jet, but she was sure they would understand when they knew. And she would have to tell them soon. She and Bear couldn't keep up this pretence for ever. They had both agreed that, if nothing happened by the time of Mia and Jet's wedding, they would give up the charade, and tell everyone they had decided to be friends.

But Alexia did keep giving the two of them odd glances every time she saw them cuddling, or laughing, or wrapped in each other's arms. She clearly had no idea it was all an act. So perhaps it was having some effect on her.

Garrick, on the other hand, looked more disgusted than jealous. Every time he saw Breanna holding hands with Bear, or whispering in Bear's ear, or watching Bear play rugby, he merely looked away. Or walked away if he could. He clearly didn't care that she might be falling in love with Bear. Not that she was. And Bear wasn't falling in love with her.

When Bear had come to pick her up for their first date and she had told him that it wouldn't work because she was in love with someone else, he had smiled, nodded and said: 'Join the club.'

They had sat and talked, and as they did, a plan had formed. A foolish, wishful plan but as Bear had asked her, what did they have to lose? If it didn't work, they would simply be in the same positions they were. But if it did. If Bear could make Alexia see him as a warm and loving partner instead of the lovesick, desperate fool he had become; if he could make her wish she hadn't dumped him all that time ago, there might be a chance.

And if Breanna could make Garrick see her as a sensual, sexy, fun loving woman instead of a walking disaster zone, perhaps he might look at her for once, instead of walking away the moment she appeared. He might never love her, but was it possible to make him see her as a grown up, and not completely unattractive, woman, and not a six-year-old girl?

The rap on the front door startled her. She wasn't expecting anyone. Her fingers caught the side of her glass which tipped over and spilt chilled white wine on the bundle of files still on the table from her evening with Mia and Ella, going over things for Mia's wedding.

'Damn it.' She jumped to her feet, grabbed a handful of tissues from the box beside her and mopped up as best she could, while the rapping continued. 'It's open,' she yelled, dashing to the kitchen to get a roll of paper towel. 'Come in.'

The door opened, she glanced up for a second but continued mopping for a moment until realisation dawned.

'Garrick? What're you doing here? Ella didn't leave her bag again, did she?'

'What? No. I have no idea.' He frowned at her. 'There's something I need to say. Will you please stop patting those files.'

She looked up and met his eyes. Something in them made her hesitate but she resumed her mopping up.

'I spilt my wine when you knocked. This is Mia's wedding stuff. I've got to soak it up.'

'Oh. Can I help?'

'No. Sit down. I'll be with you in a moment.'

'I'd rather stand.'

'Fine. Help yourself to wine.' She nodded towards the bottle. 'Grab a glass from the kitchen.'

'I'm fine.'

'Whatever. Is Flora with Alexia?'

'No. She's with Gill.'

'Gill? Where's Ella?'

'Sleeping off the wine she drank tonight. Gill's looking after both of them.'

'Oh. Gill's lovely. And extremely sensible.'

She took longer than she needed, fully aware that his stare was firmly fixed on her. An army of invisible ants raced up her body, or so it seemed and she had a feeling she might not like what Garrick had come to say.

'He is. I think you've got it all.' He sounded a little impatient. 'Breanna. Look at me. Please look at me.'

Did he just call her by her full name? This was even more serious than she thought. Oh God. He hadn't come to tell her the news she dreaded, had he? But why would he make a point of telling her? Especially at ten p.m. If he and Alexia were getting engaged, she would hear about it through the grapevine soon enough.

'Okay. Let me just throw this in the bin. Can I get you anything? A cup of coffee? A soft drink?'

'I'm fine. I just want to say what I've come to say.'

She held up one finger to ask him to give her a moment, took the sodden paper towel to the kitchen, together with her wine glass and gulped down what was left. She should've grabbed the bottle. Taking a deep breath, she returned to the sitting room and forced a friendly smile.

'I'm all yours.'

His brows shot up, his eyes grew wide and he quickly closed his open mouth.

'That seems unlikely.' He pulled a strange face. 'But I think there's something you should know. I don't think you should be dating Bear.'

Now her brows shot skywards; she blinked and didn't attempt to close her mouth.

'Excuse me?'

He ran a hand through his hair and sighed. 'I shouldn't have been so blunt. But it's true. You shouldn't be dating Bear.'

'So you said. Would you mind telling me why?'

'Because you've got nothing in common. Because he's not right for you.'

'For your information, we do have things in common.'

'Like what?'

'Like … er. We both like animals.'

'Everyone likes animals.'

'Not everyone.'

'Fine. But most people. What else?'

'Um. We both like walking.'

He rolled his eyes.

'Don't roll your eyes at me. We do both like walking. What's wrong with that?'

'It's hardly the basis for a serious relationship.'

A tiny burst of laughter escaped her. 'Who said we're having a serious relationship? We're merely having fun.'

'Oh, don't I know it. The entire village is talking about how much *fun* you and Bear are having.'

She lifted her chin, put her shoulders back and straightened her body.

'Good. I'm glad we're giving the village something to talk about.'

He glowered at her.

'I'm not sure Madeleine would be so pleased.'

'Seriously? You're throwing my mum at me.' She shook her head and laughed. 'What exactly have you got against Bear?'

'Nothing. I like him. We're friends.'

Her laughter died in her throat. 'So it's me? It's me you have a problem with? What? You don't think I'm good enough for Bear?'

'You're way too good for Bear. But it's not about that.'

'Then what *is* it about? I have no idea what you're talking about, Garrick. And even less idea why you feel you have the right to come and lecture me on my love life at ten o'clock at night.'

'Someone needs to.'

'Do they? Why? Well, it certainly shouldn't be you. Bear and I aren't the only ones the village is talking about. They've got quite a lot to say about you. Talk about having fun. You and Alexia should get a trophy for it.'

He scowled. 'Me and Alexia? The village isn't talking about me and Alexia.'

'Oh, yes it is. You're virtually inside each other's pockets. You can't take your eyes off one another. We're all waiting for the announcement.'

'Announcement? What announcement?'

'That you and Alexia are engaged.' She hadn't meant to shout that, but her anger was getting the better of her.

'That … What?' He suddenly burst out laughing. 'Is that really what people are saying? Is that honestly what people think? Is that what *you* think?'

'Well … Yes. It would be difficult to think otherwise. It's all I ever think about. You and bloody Alexia.'

Dear God. Had she just said that? Perhaps he hadn't heard it.

'All … You … Ever … Think about?'

He looked her up and down, his laughter petered out but a hint of a smile tugged at his lips as his gaze fixed firmly on her and he took a slow but meaningful step closer.

And another.

And another.

Until he stood directly in front of her.

She stared at the ground. Why couldn't she move? Why couldn't she turn away?

His voice was soft when he said her name. 'Bree? Are you saying what I think you're saying?'

Was there something under her shoes? Glue or something? Why the hell couldn't she move? She stared at her feet and shrugged her shoulders instead.

'Bree? Are you jealous? Do you have feelings for me? Bree? Why won't you look at me?'

'I don't want to.'

Well, that was intelligent. More the sort of thing a six-year-old would say, not a woman of thirty-four.

His finger lifted her chin until her eyes met his.

'Why not? I want to look at you.'

She blinked repeatedly as his face came closer and when he kissed her on the lips she couldn't stop her sigh as her eyelids fluttered closed.

It only lasted for a couple of seconds but in that short time, she could tell he wanted her as much as she wanted him, and when they moved apart she saw her surprise mirrored in his eyes.

She turned and walked away.

He sucked in an agonising breath. 'Okay. I'm sorry. I suppose I deserve that.'

'Deserve what?' Her voice still quivered a little from the softness of his lips and the sensations swirling inside her.

He ran a hand through his hair. 'Deserve you to walk away. But this is your home. If anyone should leave, it should be me.'

She smiled and continued to the door. 'Oh, I'm not leaving, Garrick. And neither are you.' She turned the lock and slid the bolt. 'And I'm not walking away. Quite the opposite, in fact.' She glanced towards the ceiling and nodded to the corner of the sitting room.

He gulped visibly as his eyes shot upwards then over to the open door leading upstairs.

'The opposite? You mean …?' His voice trailed off as his Adam's apple rose and fell and rose again.

She nodded. 'That's exactly what I mean.'

'I … I haven't been sleeping with Alexia.' There was a hint of panic in his voice.

'I don't care about Alexia.' She walked slowly towards him.

'What I mean is … I haven't slept with anyone. Not since, Fiona.'

'I understand.' She stood in front of him and looked up into his eyes. 'Are you saying it's too soon?'

He licked his lips and ran his hand through his hair again.

'Because if it is, I'll wait. I'll wait for as long as it takes. But you kissed me, remember?'

He nodded. 'I had to. I've been wanting to do that since that first night I came here.'

'You have?'

'I have.'

'But … You've been avoiding me for weeks. I don't understand.'

'I had to. Because I knew if I didn't, I would do what I've just done.'

'Kiss me, you mean?'

'And possibly a lot more besides.'

'But you and Alexia?'

'We're friends. Merely friends. She reminds me of Fiona. They look so much alike. That's why I dated her last year. But I fell in love with Mia, so I ended it. I'll admit, it crossed my mind. She's good with Flora. And I believe she is a genuinely nice person, all things considered. But she's not the one for me. And this time I fell in love with someone else. I fell in love with you.'

'With me?' This was incredible. Unbelievable. Wonderful. A miracle. 'You're saying you're in love with me?'

He nodded. 'Completely. Utterly. Insanely. That's why I couldn't stand seeing you with Bear. If I thought it was what you wanted and that you'd make each other happy, perhaps I could have borne it. Although I don't think I could've stayed in the village if you two became serious. But the thing is, Bree. I think Bear's actually in love with Alexia. And they're perfect for each other. Alexia simply doesn't realise it.'

'You love me?' She still couldn't get her head around this.

He looked into her eyes, reached out and cupped her face with his hands. 'I love you.'

'Oh, Garrick. You have no idea how much I've longed to hear you say that. I love you too.'

He smiled. 'I think I'd worked that out when you locked the door and nodded towards the bedroom.'

'Oh? That didn't necessarily indicate I loved you. I might have just wanted a bit of fun.'

He grinned. 'Excuse me. I think you mean a lot of fun. But no. The look in your eyes didn't say fun. It said love.'

She smiled and leant towards him. 'Then why the hesitation now?'

He took her in his arms and looked her in the eye. 'Because I don't want to mess this up. My love life's been a bit of a disaster area for the last year or so.'

'I'm a walking disaster area. At least I was. Things seem to be going quite well, give or take the odd hiccup, since I've been here.' She smiled at him. 'And now they're going very well. I don't think either of us should worry about messing this up. Perhaps it's time we both took a risk.'

'I'm just worried it's too soon. After Fiona, I mean.'

'I understand. You're worried what people might think. What they might say.'

'I couldn't give a damn what people think. Or what they might say. I'm not worried about that. I'm worried I might put too much pressure on you. I've got Flora to think about. She means the world to me. I wasn't sure how you feel about that.'

'How I feel about Flora? I'll tell you exactly how I feel about Flora. When I held her in my arms that day in Sunbeam Cottage, it felt right. It felt natural. It felt as if she could be mine. I'm sorry if that's the wrong thing to say. It's simply how I felt. I think I fell in love with her on the spot. I don't know if I would be a good mum. Or even if you'd want me in that role. But I can promise you this. I would love her as much as I love you. And that's a lot, in case you're in any doubt.'

'It's not the wrong thing to say. It's precisely what I hoped. And you're right about that day in Sunbeam Cottage. I saw it too. I could see us together as a family, you, me and Flora. And it terrified the life out of me for a second or two. I hadn't seen you for seventeen years, and suddenly there you are. And it felt as though no one else apart from you and Flora, mattered. I had no idea how to handle that. Or what to do about it. I told myself I had to avoid you. That my feelings weren't real. That it was some sort of rebound. That in a week or two I'd laugh at my stupidity. But all I could think about was you. And when I saw you in Jenny's bakery and felt your touch as you wiped off all that water, it was all I could do to stop myself from pulling you into my arms and kissing you right then and there.'

'I don't know what to say.'

He smiled. 'Perhaps we've done enough talking.' He glanced towards the stairs. 'Maybe it is time we found other ways to express our feelings for each other. I'm just a bit nervous.'

'I'm nervous too. Let's just see how it goes, shall we? There's no rush.'

He nodded and his smile grew wider. 'I like the sound of that.'

She returned his smile, slipped her hand in his and didn't say another word as they walked towards the stairs.

Chapter Twenty-Two

'Bear's here on his own,' Mia said, the following evening, glancing towards the bar of The Frog and Lily and nudging Ella's arm. 'I wonder where Bree is tonight.'

'Perhaps she's in the loo. For the past couple of weeks, wherever one is, the other's not far away.'

Mia smiled. 'I know. It's quite surprising, isn't it? They really seem to be getting on well together. But when I ask her about him, she goes all coy and tight-lipped.'

'Yeah. I've noticed that. And she gets a strange little smile on her face. As if she knows something the rest of us don't.'

'If they're sleeping together, she does know something the rest of us don't. She knows what he's like in bed.'

'That's true. Have you ever wondered about that? What Bear's like in bed, I mean?'

Mia laughed. 'No. I can honestly say it's never been high on my list of things I'd like to know.'

'Not even when you dated him?'

'Oddly enough, especially *not* when I dated him. As we've said before, he was a bit OTT.'

'Yeah. He's probably one of those guys who talks all the way through it. You know? Offers words of encouragement. Things like, "right there, baby", or "you're doing great", or "is that good for you?" Stuff like that.'

'Yes. Thank you. You've given me a very clear picture.' Mia rolled her eyes.

'He's got a good body though.'

'It's a good thing Gill can't hear you saying this.' She nodded to the bar where Gill and Jet were now chatting with Bear.

Ella grinned. 'There's no harm in wondering. I don't fancy Bear. I merely like to know these things. It's good for an editor to have an enquiring mind. I adore Gill. I'd never dream of cheating on him.'

'That's good to know.'

Jet and Gill returned, drinks in hand, and gave Mia and Ella each a large glass of wine.

'You might want to consider calling Bree when we get home,' Jet said.

'Is she ill?'

Jet and Gill exchanged looks.

'No.' Jet sat beside Mia. 'But it seems the romance is over.' He nodded towards Bear who still sat alone at the bar.

'Between Bree and Bear?' Mia darted a look at Ella.

Jet nodded. 'Bear just told us. He said they're really good friends, but they've decided to call it a day. I told him he was welcome to join us, but he says he's got some thinking to do.'

Ella frowned. 'They were getting on so well. Mia and I were just talking about that.'

'It didn't stand a chance,' said Gill. 'They're obviously both in love with other people.'

'Bear's in love with Alexia, you mean?' asked Mia.

Both Gill and Jet nodded.

'And Bree's in love with Garrick.' Jet sighed, shook his head and sipped his pint.

'How did you know that?' Mia asked. 'I never said a word. I promised Bree I wouldn't.'

Jet tutted. 'Keeping secrets, eh? But I'll let you off. I know, because I've seen the way she behaves when someone mentions Garrick's name, or, during the last couple of weeks, how she acted with Bear whenever Garrick was around. And I use the word, 'acted' literally.'

Mia gasped. 'What? Are you saying you think her relationship with Bear was all an act? That it was fake?'

'Yep.'

'What about Bear? Was he also acting?'

'I'd put money on it. If I were a gambling man. Which of course, I'm not.'

'But why?' Ella queried. 'What was the point?'

Gill piped up. 'Perhaps to see if either of them could make Alexia and Garrick jealous.'

'Well, good luck with that,' Ella said. 'Sadly, Garrick couldn't be less interested in Bree if he tried. Every time I mention her name, he walks away or changes the subject.'

Jet eyed her over the rim of his beer glass. 'Are you sure about that? That he's not interested in Bree, I mean. Because I've seen the way he looks at her, especially since she's been dating Bear and a man doesn't look at a woman in that way if he's not interested.'

'I think I know my brother.'

'Do you? Have you asked him?'

'Of course not. He's been seeing Alexia. I'm not going to come right out and ask him if he fancies Bree.'

'That's unusually diplomatic of you,' Jet said, grinning. 'You usually say what you think, regardless.'

'Fine. I'll ask him tonight when we get home.'

'Where is he this evening?'

'At home. Looking after Flora.'

'Are you also sure about that?'

'Yes, Jet. I am.'

Jet grinned. 'Then why did Pete tell me when we first walked in here that he saw Garrick's van heading down Farm Lane in the direction of Willow Cottage? He asked me if Garrick had got a new battery yet because the last time he was down that way, his van wouldn't start and Pete had to jump start it.'

Ella looked at Mia and they both gave a little shriek.

'No way,' said Mia.

'I'll kill him,' Ella said.

'Why?' Gill asked. 'You like Bree. So what's the problem?'

'The problem is, he should've told me.'

'Why?'

'Because I'm his sister. His twin sister. We tell each other everything.'

'Apparently not,' Jet said. 'But there's nothing wrong with that. Perhaps he wants a bit of privacy. After everything that's happened, that's completely understandable. Or perhaps Bree doesn't want him to say anything. Although they may not be dating yet. Just because he's going to see her, it doesn't mean they're jumping into bed together.'

'What's he done with Flora?' Ella got to her feet. 'I'd better go and see.'

Gill grabbed her hand and pulled her back down. 'You'll do no such thing. If Garrick's gone to Bree's you can be sure he's either taken Flora with him, or he's left her with someone capable of taking care of her.'

'Well, he hasn't left Flora with Alexia,' Mia said, 'because she's just walked in. Alone, I might add. I think I'll go and have a word.'

'Mi-a,' Jet said, but he was grinning.

'What? I want to ask her something about the wedding.'

'Of course you do.' Jet nodded, his grin growing wider. 'You shouldn't lie to your fiancé, you know. It might make him feel anxious.'

'Oh poo and nonsense. And I say that with love, my darling.'

Mia stood up, kissed Jet on the cheek and glanced at Ella, indicating that Ella should go with her. They followed Alexia to the bar, hesitating for a split second when Alexia took a seat beside Bear.

'What do we do now?' Ella whispered.

'Let's stand here.' Mia grabbed Ella's sleeve and led her to the wide, wooden upright post, less than half a metre away from where Bear and Alexia sat, but large enough for Mia and Ella to hide behind, in spite of them getting some rather curious looks from some of the other customers nearby. 'But try to look casual. Like we're just chatting.'

Ella grinned at Mia. 'As opposed to eavesdropping, you mean?'

'Hello,' Alexia said to Bear. 'I'm surprised to see you here on your own. Where's your shadow tonight? Sorry. I meant, where's Bree?'

There was laughter in her voice and Bear laughed too.

'No idea. We've called it a day. No pun intended.'

'Well, well, Rupert Bear Day. What are we going to do with you? Do any of your relationships last longer than a fortnight? Have you taken over Jet's mantle? Date as many women as you can, dump them and run. In the nicest possible way, obviously.' She laughed louder.

'Bloody cheek,' whispered Mia.

'She does have a point,' said Ella. 'Even Jet admits he did that before he met you.'

'Shush. I'm trying to listen. It's difficult enough to hear with all the noise in here without you talking as well.'

Bear smiled sardonically. 'It's not a cunning plan on my part. It just seems to be the way things work out. You can't pretend to be in love with someone if you're not.'

Alexia nodded. 'I completely agree. The trouble with you and me is we keep dating the wrong people.'

Bear fiddled with his beer glass. 'Not always.'

'What's that supposed to mean? If we dated the right people we wouldn't still be single.'

'We would if one of us fell for the right person, but that person dumped them for someone else.'

'What? That made no sense at all. Neither one of us has ever fallen for the right person. Although we've both been dumped by people several times.'

'Haven't we? I fell for you, Alexia, hook, line and sinker, but you dumped me for Jet, remember? And he subsequently dumped you, by which time I was drowning my sorrows with someone else. I asked you out again but you told me not to be so bloody ridiculous.'

Alexia stared at him. 'Did I? When? I don't remember that at all. I suppose I was still angry with Jet and I took it out on you.'

'How do you feel about Jet now?'

'That he's a friend. A good friend. But nothing more. Not that it would matter. Because there will never be anyone else for Jet now that he's met Mia.'

Mia nudged Ella and smiled triumphantly.

Ella tutted. 'Oh, do shut up. I'm listening.'

Bear gulped his beer. 'Can I buy you a drink?'

Alexia nodded. 'Yes, please. Red wine. I'll get it. It's getting busy in here tonight.' She went behind the bar, waved at her brother Toby, pulled another pint for Bear and poured herself a large glass of wine, returning to her seat and smiling as she clinked glasses with Bear.

'And Garrick? Where's he tonight?' Bear asked.

'Don't know.'

'But you're still dating?'

Alexia coughed on a mouthful of wine. 'We're not dating. I thought we might. If I'm honest, when I first saw him, shortly after he came back, I hoped we would. But it clearly wasn't meant to be.'

'How do you feel about that? About him?'

She shrugged. 'A friend, too, I suppose. For a while I convinced myself I was falling in love with him, but I think it was Flora I was falling in love with. Although, not really her either. More the idea of being a mum. Of having a family. Of settling down. Oh, I don't know. I've made such a mess of things. I'm not sure anyone will really get over what I said and did last year. I'm not sure I'll ever get over it. But I wish I could. I just want to be … loved, I think. You know? To be really special to one particular person. To mean the world to them and for them to mean the world to me. I suppose I want what Mia and Jet have. And what Ella and Gill, and now Toby and Christy, and Cathy and Leo, and Lori and Franklin. And my mum and dad, of course. Even Hettie and Fred have that. Is it too much to ask to have it too?' She laughed mirthlessly. 'I think I'll be single for the rest of my life.'

Bear cleared his throat and looked Alexia in the eye, and from their position behind the post, Mia and Ella exchanged open mouthed glances.

'You don't need to be,' Bear said. 'Single, I mean. And you are really special to one particular person. You mean the world to them. I know you don't feel the same way, but maybe in time you could. Possibly?'

She met his eyes as he put down his glass and reached out to brush a lock of hair from her face.

'What are you saying, Bear?' Her voice crackled with anticipation.

'I'm saying, nothing's changed. You're still the right one for me, Alexia, and I think you always will be. Even when you thumped that policeman and turned into some kind of demented banshee, deep down, I still thought you were wonderful.'

She gave a nervous laugh. 'Really?'

He nodded. 'Really.'

'You mean it? You're not just saying this? You're not just trying to get me into bed, are you?'

'Alexia. You know me better than that. I might do that with other women. But I wouldn't do that with you. If we didn't sleep together for a year it wouldn't matter to me. Well, it would matter, and I'd want to. I'd definitely want to. But I'd happily wait until it was what you wanted too. However long that took.'

'So … are you asking me out? Are you asking me to be your girlfriend? Are you saying we might have a future together?'

'I am. Yes to all three. Don't you think we could? Build a future together, I mean.'

She looked at him for several seconds until a smile lit up her face and eyes. 'Do you know what? I think perhaps we could. I only ended things with you because I was so besotted with Jet. But if he hadn't been around, I think things might have worked between us.'

He smiled and there was laughter in his voice. 'So, providing no one else like Jet Cross comes along, are you willing to give it a try? To take a chance on me?'

'Even if someone like Jet comes along, it wouldn't matter. I've learnt that particular lesson. I've learnt a few other lessons, too.'

'I think we've all done that. It's a yes, then?' He held out his hand towards her.

She smiled and slipped her hand into his. 'It's a yes. Rupert Bear Day, you've got yourself a girlfriend.'

'Hallelujah,' he said, leaning forward and pulling her towards him.

He kissed her on the lips, and Mia and Ella, and everyone else in the pub cheered and clapped and whooped with joy. Both Alexia and Bear were blushing when they eased apart. But not too far apart.

'It's about bloody time,' said Freda, from behind the bar. 'But you watch it, Bear. If you hurt my girl, you'll have me to answer to.

'And me,' said Toby, marching over and slapping Bear on the back.

Jet and Gill joined Mia and Ella, and Jet went to Bear, gave him a manly hug, and also hugged Alexia.

'I was beginning to think this would never happen. Good luck to both of you.'

'Let's hope this time my girlfriend's here to stay,' said Bear.

Alexia smiled and leant closer to him. 'After that kiss, I think it's pretty much a certainty. But I'm not sure it'll be smooth sailing. People will tell you, your girlfriend can be a bit of a bitch.'

She laughed and everyone laughed with her.

Bear pulled her back into his arms. 'I wouldn't have her any other way. I love her just the way she is.'

This time when they kissed, they ignored the cheers and whoops of joy, and Mia nudged Ella and grinned.

'I've said it before and I'll say it again. There's definitely something magical about Little Pondale.'

Chapter Twenty-Three

Mia and Ella had agreed with Jet and Gill that they wouldn't ask either Breanna or Garrick if the pair of them were dating.

'We should leave it up to them to tell us,' Jet had said in the pub on that Saturday night. 'They may want to see how things go before they make it public. Assuming they are dating that is, and they're not merely friends.'

'But this is Little Pondale,' Ella had argued. 'Everyone will find out sooner or later, and if Hettie gets wind of it, it'll definitely be sooner. When I tell Garrick about Alexia and Bear, he'll probably tell me anyway.'

'Then wait and see if he does,' said Gill. 'But if he doesn't, don't push him. Give him time.'

'Fine.'

'Okay,' agreed Mia.

On Sunday morning, Ella phoned Mia. 'Garrick was in bed last night when we got home but by the time I got up, he'd already left. He told

Gill that he and Flora were going out for the day, and probably wouldn't be back till late.'

'Did Gill ask him where?'

Ella tutted. 'No. And when I moaned at him, he told me that it wasn't really any of our business. If Garrick wanted us to know, he'd tell us.'

'Men. They simply don't understand. What if you need to get in touch with Garrick for some reason?'

'That's exactly the argument I used. But Gill simply rolled his eyes and continued eating his toast. Are you seeing Bree tomorrow?'

'No. Not for a couple of days. She's meeting some new clients. She's not going to be at choir practice on Tuesday, either. There was a message on the landline when we got home last night. She said that Delphinie would like me to go for my fitting this Wednesday, so Bree needs to do a few last-minute things on Tuesday evening. She's suggested we go to the station together on Wednesday morning to get the train to London. That's me, Mum, you and Bree. Tiffany will meet us there. You and she can try on your bridesmaids' dresses in case there're any alterations needed.'

'Damn. I might pop into Willow Cottage before then, just to say hello.'

'No you won't. Not without me. And I promised Jet I wouldn't interfere. So did you.'

'Yeah. But I lied. It's my brother, Mia. I need to know one way or the other.'

'I know you do. But Jet and Gill may have a point. Garrick has suffered a terrible loss, he's got a baby to look after, his grief to deal with, and he hasn't seen Bree for years. Perhaps we should give them some time. Imagine if everyone knew they were dating and it only lasted a week. Things might get awkward. And from a purely selfish viewpoint, I have got my wedding to think about. As my best friend, so have you.'

'Okay. Fine.'

'Good. Now on the subject of my wedding, I need some advice. I still haven't decided who'll walk me down the aisle. I was thinking of going it alone, with you and Tiffany walking behind me, but the more I think about it, the more I want to ask Mum to do it. I've discussed it with Jet and he likes the idea. What do you think?'

'D'you really need to ask? Lori would love it. In a way, it'll feel as if your dad's with you. Oh, don't get me all emotional. Gill's taking me out for Sunday lunch and I don't want to start crying and end up all blotchy.' Ella gave a little cough. 'What about Prince Gustav? If he was good enough for Hettie's wedding, he's good enough for yours.'

Mia laughed. 'I did think about him. But I'll go with Mum. I'll pop round to see her later and ask. Jet still hasn't chosen his best man. It's between Toby and Bear but he can't decide because he doesn't want to pick one over the other.'

'He hasn't got long.'

'I know. Five weeks, minus one day. I told him if he still can't decide by the beginning of May, he should get them to draw straws. That way neither one can take offence. The problem is, I think the person he really wanted is Justin.'

'Justin? My ex, Justin.'

Mia laughed. 'He was Jet's best friend for more than thirty-four years. You dated him for one summer. But yes, Justin Lake.'

'Did he say no?'

'Jet didn't ask him. He says Justin's got too much on his plate, what with his filming schedule, TV interviews, and jetting off all over the world. Jet didn't say that bit. That was me. He did send him an invitation, and Justin's said yes. But that it might just be a fleeting visit.'

'Getting a bit too big for his boots, eh?'

'It certainly sounds that way. Even Jenny doesn't hear from him much, and he's her cousin.'

'It might be better if Justin didn't turn up. The last thing you want is a Hollywood star at your wedding. He'll steal the limelight. And if the paparazzi got wind of it, the village would be swarming with press. Could you imagine how awful that would be?'

'Oddly enough, that was another reason Jet was loath to ask him to be his best man. And when Justin phoned to congratulate us on setting the date, I heard Jet tell him that we didn't want any fuss. Justin must have understood because when he briefly spoke to me, he assured me he'd be incognito.'

'In Cognito? Is that in Mexico?' Ella said, laughing.

'Oh ha ha.'

'Speaking of Justin, we need to sort out your hen night. Are The Frog Hill Hounds still performing? I know they weren't the same after Justin left, but still. Hunky men taking off their clothes to music – what's not to like?'

Mia giggled. 'I'll ask Hettie. She's bound to know. Although I don't think she goes to many of those meetings since she married Fred. And I'm not sure I want a hen night like that. I was thinking more of a day at one of those posh, expensive spas, followed by cocktails, dinner and a show.'

'When did you turn eighty? Spa, yes. Cocktails and dinner, yes. Replace show with all-night dance club and you're on.'

'I'm not sure Mum and Hettie, or me for that matter, could dance all night, but okay. I'll get Bree on to it. We'll have limos to take us there and back. I'd better find out who wants to come.'

'Are you mad? Everybody will. You'll have to decide who to invite.'

'That sounds like another job for Bree. I'm so glad we bumped into her.'

'Yeah. Me too. And so, it might seem, is Garrick.'

Chapter Twenty-Four

The fittings went well and Mia was thrilled with her dress. It was beautiful, exceeding her expectations and more flattering than she had hoped. Delphinie was both a talented designer and an expert seamstress, and her team of sewers, lace makers and embroiderers were all involved in creating and producing what was effectively a work of art.

Ella and Tiffany's bridesmaids' dresses required little alteration and, after lunch, an unscheduled shopping spree followed by early evening cocktails, Mia, Lori, Ella and Breanna wished Tiffany farewell and caught the train home from London, relaxed but elated, tired and a teensy bit tipsy.

'How's your dress?' Jet asked, when Mia finally returned to Little Pond Farm around eight p.m.

'It's magnificent, fabulous, breathtakingly beautiful and exactly what I dreamt of.'

'That's how I feel about you.' He winked at her and smiled, kissing her on the lips. 'I can't wait to see you in it. I can't wait to see you out of it afterwards. I wonder if we'll feel different making love as husband and wife.'

'I don't know. But perhaps we'd better make the most of the time we've got while we're still unmarried. Just in case.'

'Absolutely. And there's no time like the present. Oh, but I've got news.'

'Good news?'

'Very good news. I've got my best man.'

'Excellent. Toby or Bear.'

'Justin.'

'Justin?'

'Yep. We had a long chat earlier this evening. He said he's been thinking a lot about us since he got our invitation, and he suddenly realised that he had lost sight of his priorities. That Hollywood is great, but it's definitely not Little Pondale.'

'He had to think about that? Anyone could have told him Little Pondale isn't Hollywood.'

'I think he meant as far as friendship is concerned. Anyway, the outcome was he's definitely coming to the wedding and he asked who I'd chosen as my best man. I said I hadn't, but that if he had been here it would've been him. He said if I wanted him to be, it would be both an honour and a pleasure. He also said he'll come the day before but will do a detour to throw off any press.' Jet grinned. 'And he'll wear a disguise until we're inside the church.'

'You're really pleased it's him, aren't you?'

'Yeah. Toby and Bear are great, but I always felt closer to Justin. I miss him sometimes. I'd miss him more, if I didn't have you. I'm happy for him though, and thrilled with his success. But I think that one day, he may very well return to Little Pondale.'

'It's a difficult place to leave. I don't think I could ever move.'

'I'll never let you.'

'I'm serious. I love it here. And it really is a magical place. I told Bree that when she first came here. I told her people find happiness and have their dreams come true, and that she would do the same. And she has, hasn't she? Her business is taking off and will clearly be a huge success. She's happy living in Willow Cottage. And, if it's true about her and Garrick, she's even found love, too. And so has he.'

'That's true. Did she say anything today?'

'Nope. Not a word. In spite of Ella trying everything she could to get her to say something.'

'She'll tell you when she's ready. They both will.'

They walked arm in arm towards the stairs.

'I hope it works out between them. Garrick deserves to be happy. They both do. But isn't life odd? They've known each other since they were six, but they never got together. And then they see each other again and within a couple of months, they're dating. And who knows where that may lead?'

'Well, in theory only one of two ways. They'll either go their separate ways, or they'll stay together.'

'Yes but … Oh. My. God!' Mia stopped in her tracks.

'What?'

'The fortune-teller.'

Jet gave her an odd look. 'The fortune-teller?'

'Yes. The one at the Summer Fête. I've got to phone Ella.' She turned and hesitated, deciding which room to call her from.

'I thought we were going to bed.'

'I can't go to bed now. This is huge. This is so exciting. It's unbelievable.'

'Er. Perhaps you could fill me in before you phone Ella?'

'You won't believe it. She will.'

'Try me.'

'Okay. Let's go into the sitting room. I'll phone her from there.'

He sighed and followed her to the sofa, taking a seat beside her.

'I'm all ears.'

She gave him a playful shove. 'You're making a joke of it already and I haven't even told you what the fortune-teller said. She's been right about everyone, so far, but we thought she'd got it totally wrong about Garrick. But she hasn't. And if she's got it right, our wedding won't be the only one on Lily Pond Lane this year.'

'What? Are you telling me that Bree and Garrick will get married? This year?'

'Yes. Why not? We had a whirlwind romance. So did Mum and Franklin. And Ella and Gill. Not forgetting Hettie and Fred.'

'And Cathy and Leo. And Toby and Christy. And Alexia and Bear.' He grinned at her.

'You're making fun of me again.'

He took her hands in his and smiled. 'I'm not. You're right. Lots of people have fallen in love very quickly in Little Pondale. But what has this got to do with the fortune-teller?'

'I need to remember what she said.' Mia racked her brains. 'Okay. I've got it. I think. She told Garrick that he'd met the woman of his dreams and that they'd have a lifetime of happiness together with a large family. But that she saw two women in his life. Oh. That bit's irrelevant. That's what threw us off. But we figured that out. Anyway, she also said that she heard a child's heartbeat. That he had to make a choice. No wait. That bit's old news too. This is the next part that's important. She saw a wedding and the saying "marry in haste, repent at leisure" wouldn't apply. If he married in haste, he would find true pleasure. True happiness. Providing he made the right choice. That's it.'

'Er. As fascinating as that is, are you saying that Garrick should marry Bree because a fortune-teller said he would find true happiness if he married in haste?'

'Yes. And that he'd already met the woman of his dreams. Well, that must be Bree, mustn't it? Don't forget, Jet. This was the same fortune-teller who told Mattie that she should try and bring us together. And look what's happened to us.'

He pulled a face. 'Okay. That's true. Well, in that case, it won't be long before Bree's planning her own wedding. Now can we go to bed?'

'Not yet, no. I told you. I've got to phone Ella.'

'Why? So that she can tell Garrick?'

'Yes.'

'Can't it wait until tomorrow? One night's not going to make much difference.'

'But it's exciting!'

'And going to bed with me isn't? Thanks.' He shook his head and laughed. 'Give Ella my love. I'll see you upstairs once the two of you have thought up some cunning plan to make sure Garrick and Bree get married.'

She watched him walk towards the door before glancing at the phone.

Jet was right. What difference would one night make?

'Wait for me, Jet. I'll call Ella first thing in the morning.' She jumped to her feet and ran to him.

Laughing, he swept her up in his arms and carried her upstairs.

Chapter Twenty-Five

Breanna couldn't believe her ears when Garrick told
her the following evening about the fortune-teller at the Summer Fête last year.

'I'm sorry, Garrick but could you repeat that please? Because I think I must've misheard you.'

Garrick ran a hand through his hair and leant on the back of the chair in the sitting room of Willow Cottage.

'It sounds ridiculous I know. But everything that fortune-teller said has come true so far. Not just for me. For everyone who had their fortune told that day. I'd forgotten all about it until Ella reminded me today. But don't you see? It makes perfect sense.'

'Does it? She said you'd met the woman of your dreams. Are you saying that's me?'

'I haven't been able to stop thinking about you since the moment I saw you again on that first night you arrived. And you must admit, our first night in bed together was pretty sensational. And every night – and day, since, has been wonderful. So yes.'

'That's true. That's definitely true. So … she said that if you marry in haste, you'll find true happiness? Are you … are you suggesting we get married?'

'Yes. Well, no. Not immediately. Not right away. Haste can mean anything.'

'Haste usually means quickly.'

'Within a year, perhaps.'

'We've just started dating.'

'You said you loved me.'

'I do love you, Garrick.'

'Then … If you love me, what's the problem?'

'The problem is that you would only be asking me because some woman in a tent at a Summer Fête charged you a fee and told you a story.'

'A story? It's all come true.'

'Perhaps people have made it come true. That's what you're doing now. Or trying to. You're trying to make a situation fit her prediction.'

'No. I'm saying her prediction fits our situation. I love you, Bree. I think we could have a future together. I know we could. And believe me, I didn't expect this. After Fiona died, I didn't think I'd ever fall in love again. Unless it was unrequited love for Mia. I had tunnel vision. I couldn't see anything ahead but sorrow and loneliness as far as love was concerned. I thought friendship was my only option. Until that night I saw you, and my heart virtually exploded out of my chest. We could be a family, Bree. You, me and Flora.' He smiled lovingly at her. 'And according to the fortune-teller, Flora won't be our only child. She said we'd have a lifetime of happiness together with a large family.'

Breanna turned away. 'Well, that's where I can prove her wrong. Or at least prove that I'm not the one who will give you a lifetime of happiness and a large family.'

'What? Why not? Don't you want children? You love Flora.'

She turned back to look at him, tears welling up in her eyes. 'I do love Flora. Very much. And I would love to have children. Lots and lots of children. But the thing is, Garrick. I can't. There's a problem with my ovaries. To quote the specialist I saw many years ago when I was having severe stomach cramps. I stand more chance of winning the lottery than I do of having a child. Not even a fortune-teller can beat those odds.'

She swiped at the tears trickling down her cheeks and Garrick immediately went to her and took her in his arms, but it was a while before he spoke.

'I'm so sorry, Bree. I had no idea.'

'Why would you? How could you know? But don't you see? As much as I would give anything to be the woman of your dreams. The woman who could give you a lifetime of happiness and a large family. To marry you within a year. Within a month. I'd marry you tomorrow if you asked. But it's not me, Garrick. Not if you really believe that what the fortune-teller told you is the truth.'

He lifted her chin and looked her in the eyes. 'I know you think I'm crazy for believing the fortune-teller. I probably am. But I do believe it. We all do. Well, perhaps not Jet. He's as sceptical as you are. But I think it's you, Bree. I think you are the woman of my dreams. No. I don't think that. I know it. I know it in my heart. I'm more certain about this than I've ever been about anything in my life. It's you, Bree. And we could have a lifetime of happiness together. We will have a lifetime of happiness together. As for the large family. Well, we've already got Flora. And pets are family. Perhaps we'll have lots of dogs and cats.'

A snigger of laughter escaped her.

'And there's another thing you're forgetting. I don't know how you'd feel about it, but there are plenty of kids out there who need a loving home and a happy family.'

Breanna blinked several times. 'Adoption?'

He gave a small shrug of his shoulders. 'It's a possibility. A thought. That's all.'

She smiled up at him. 'It is. And it's a wonderful thought.'

He smiled down at her. 'Then I think you may have a new client to add to your list at *The Wright*

Wedding. Her name's Breanna Wright and someday soon, once Mia and Jet's wedding is done and dusted, a man who loves Breanna very much is going to ask her to marry him and from what I gather, Breanna will say yes.'

Her smile spread to her eyes as his arms tightened around her. 'I'll pencil something in right away. But I'm pretty sure I can work something out for her no matter when.'

'June sounds nice.'

Breanna gave a soft gasp. 'June sounds very nice.'

'Let's pencil something in for June. I'm pretty sure he'll get around to asking her by then. I'll mention it to Glen and see if anything's free.'

'Perhaps he won't ask her. Perhaps she'll ask him. I believe she's the kind of girl who likes to take a risk. In fact. I think she kissed someone when she was six. Yes. The more I think about this, the more I feel there's a distinct possibility she may propose to him.'

'If he doesn't ask her first. But if she does, I can promise her one thing. He definitely won't run away.'

Chapter Twenty-Six

No one in the village seemed at all surprised that Breanna and Garrick had become 'an item'.

'I could tell by the way they looked at one another,' Hettie had told anyone who would listen, including Mia and Ella. 'And Alexia resembles poor dead, Fiona far too closely for that to have been a healthy relationship. But Bree's about as opposite to Fiona as it's possible to get.'

Mia couldn't argue with that.

The month of May blossomed into sunshine, and so did the cherry trees, the magnolias and the myriad, late spring flowers. Almost every seed from the packets of sweet peas sent with the wedding invitations had germinated and by the day of Mia's hen party, a kaleidoscope of brightly coloured petals climbed up trellises or tumbled from window boxes, hanging baskets, and the like, throughout the village, and hopefully, beyond.

The hen party went exactly as Mia had planned, with a little added bonus the following evening, of a performance by The Frog Hill

Hounds, courtesy of Ella and organised by Breanna through some of Hettie's contacts at the W.I.

'This isn't just for you, it's for all of us,' Ella said, stuffing a fiver into each of the gorgeous hunks' one remaining item of clothing – G-strings, which all looked as if they were pretty full already.

Mia didn't ask whether anyone had arranged a female equivalent for Jet's bachelor party, but she trusted him completely, so she hoped he had had fun. Especially as Justin Lake had flown over unexpectedly, merely so that he could join Jet in his celebrations.

Mia hadn't recognised him when he turned up at Little Pond Farm in a beaten-up taxi.

She opened the front door to a seemingly old, stooped woman with a fair amount of dark stubble surrounding a prominent mole on a pointed chin. Huge sunglasses perched on an owl-like nose and a massive, floppy hat skewed at an angle hid a mass of bright red curls. Mia very nearly had a heart attack once the taxi drove out of sight and Justin straightened up and yelled, 'Surprise!'

The week before the wedding, everything was ready. No hiccups in sight, no cancellations, no sudden illnesses or accidents, no delays, distractions or dampening of spirits.

Thanks to Mia and to Jet, and as Mia insisted, to the woman herself, Breanna Wright had risen from the ashes of her disaster-filled life, to the pinnacle of success. *The Wright Wedding* was fast becoming the go-to name for any soon-to-be bride.

'It's nothing short of a miracle,' Breanna said, thanking Mia for the umpteenth time.

'You did all the hard work, Bree. You don't need to thank me and Jet. You need to give yourself a large pat on the back.'

Mia couldn't be happier for her. Breanna's diary was full.

But just a few days before the wedding, Breanna started being sick. She put it down to nerves. Mia told her to go and see a doctor, or to pay Bear a visit at the very least.

And Little Pondale had apparently conjured up another miracle.

Mia was surprised – and yet she wasn't. Ella was 'gob-smacked' but happy and Breanna and Garrick were deliriously, ridiculously euphoric. According to Bear, it wasn't merely Breanna's diary that was full, her belly was too. And the following day, the hospital confirmed it.

Breanna Wright and Garrick Swann were expecting twins. It was early days, of course, but the tests confirmed Breanna was carrying two healthy babies.

'But I can't be pregnant!' Breanna said, crying on Garrick's shoulder as Mia and Jet and Ella and Gill, looked on. 'It's impossible. The specialist told me years ago, I stand more chance of winning the Lottery than I do of getting pregnant.'

'People win the Lottery all the time,' Jet said.

'Nothing's impossible in Little Pondale,' Mia added. 'In this place, anything can happen. I told you that.'

'You see, my darling,' Garrick said, kissing Breanna repeatedly and laughing almost hysterically. 'I told you the fortune-teller was right. I knew that it was you.'

Later, as Mia and Jet lay in each other's arms in bed that night, discussing how incredible life could be. And how unexpected. Jet said: 'How do you feel about having one of those?'

'A set of twins?'

He laughed. 'Or triplets, or sextuplets. Or as many as you like.'

'Let's just start with one, and see how it goes from there. But let's get married first.'

'I never took you for a prude.' He kissed her on the lips.

'I'm not. But I want to drink lots of champagne at our wedding, and I can't do that if I'm pregnant. Besides, my contraceptive injection doesn't wear off for another two weeks.'

'In the middle of our honeymoon?'

'Slap bang in the middle. No pun intended.'

He kissed her neck and ran his fingers along her collar bone.

'There's not much to do on a private island in the middle of the Pacific Ocean. Apart from the odd day trip to nearby Bora Bora, or swimming in the warm, azure waters with the Manta Rays,

Dolphins and Flying Fish.' His eyes twinkled as he spoke.

Her body tingled from his touch as it always did.

'And lazing on soft sand beaches, drinking cocktails, eating coconut and freshly caught fish. But other than that, we'll have plenty of time to work on starting a family of our own.'

'Work?' Laughter mingled with passion filled his eyes.

She nodded, grinning. 'And I can be a slave-driver.'

Chapter Twenty-Seven

Several rays of bright sunlight woke Mia in the early morning of her wedding day, together with the delightful aroma of freshly made coffee, a large mug of which, Breanna brought to Mia's bedside.

'Morning. Did you sleep well?' Breanna asked, beaming. She placed the coffee on Mia's bedside table, crossed the room and threw back the curtains. 'It's such a beautiful day. Perfect weather for your wedding. Not a cloud in the sky.'

Mia propped herself up against the pillows and reached out for the coffee. 'Morning. Thanks for this. I hardly slept a wink. I know it's crazy, but I really missed Jet. And even though I know everything will run like clockwork in your capable hands, I kept waking up and wondering if we've forgotten something.'

'We haven't.' Breanna tapped the duvet covering Mia's foot. 'Trust me. Everything's fine. But we are on a bit of a tight schedule. Jet arranged a little surprise for you, so you need to come downstairs in about thirty minutes, and you might want to brush your hair.'

Mia's free hand shot to her head and she pulled a face as her fingers caught a tangle.

'A surprise? What sort of surprise? He's not here is he? It's unlucky for us to see each other before the ceremony.'

'He's not here.' She glanced at her watch. 'He'll be having a leisurely breakfast at Bear's sometime this morning, after which, he'll relax some more before getting ready for the church. As for the surprise, you'll have to come to the dining room.'

'Do I need to get dressed?'

'Only if you want to. Most people will still be in their nightwear. I'm dressed because I had to pop outside. I'm going to wake Ella and anyone else who isn't up yet and I'll see you downstairs in half an hour. Don't forget the hair. There'll no doubt be photos.'

'Photos? Photos of what?'

'Come downstairs and see.' She grinned as she closed the door behind her.

Mia sipped her coffee. What had Jet arranged? She glanced around the bedroom, bathed in golden sunshine and smiled. The birds were serenading her and a warm breeze wafted in through the open windows. She could stay here for another twenty minutes or so, according to Bree's schedule before she needed to brush her hair and get downstairs.

Who was she kidding? She gulped down her coffee, threw back the duvet, jumped out of bed and dashed to the dressing table. Ten minutes later, hair brushed, teeth cleaned and after a quick wash, she grabbed her lightweight, summer dressing gown and skipped downstairs humming along to one of the hymns from the upcoming ceremony.

The farmhouse seemed quiet, especially without Little M, who had spent the night with Jet. Lucky dog. But it was still only seven-thirty.

Mia smiled as she pushed open the dining room doors.

'Surprise!'

A cacophony of voices shouted as a harpist began playing a selection of mellow, wedding music, and champagne corks were popped by several smartly dressed waiting staff. A large, congratulatory banner together with several balloons filled the room.

The dining table was set with a selection of both hot and cold serving dishes down the centre and everyone, who had either spent last night at the farmhouse, or was involved in today's preparations stood behind each chair, with Mia's chair at one end, and Lori's at the other. Each plate had a breakfast menu with Xavier Sombeanté's iconic logo emblazoned on it and Mia and Jet's name, together with today's date was printed at the bottom – a souvenir of the morning for those involved.

Tears of happiness filled Mia's eyes. 'This is Jet's surprise?' She rubbed her temple with her hand, and flopped into her seat. 'I can't believe it. This is amazing.'

'This isn't all of it,' Breanna said, handing her a glass of champagne from one of the waiters. 'Jet arranged for Xavier and Luke to do all the catering for the entire day.'

Mia blinked in astonishment and took several gulps of champagne. 'The entire day. But what about the Bywaters? What will they say?'

'You twit,' Ella said, laughing. 'They're in on it.'

Mia glanced at Breanna, who nodded.

'They've known all along. They were very good at keeping it secret.'

'I've got to phone Jet and thank him. This is incredible.'

'Can't we eat first?' Ella asked. 'I'm starving. Although I'm disappointed there's no breakfast cereal.' She grinned at Mia and winked. 'You can phone Jet later. Besides, he's probably having a lie in.'

'He won't be. But he might be walking Little M. Okay. I'll call him later.'

There was smoked salmon, kedgeree, eggs Benedict, several different types of bread and toast, blinis, honey, conserves, fresh fruit, coffee, tea and of course, plenty of champagne.

'Don't drink too much,' Lori warned, with a grin. 'You don't want to slur your vows.'

By eight-thirty and several flashing-phone-camera-shots later, Mia was in the shower, after which she had a massage, pedicure, manicure and her hair and make-up done. Her golden brown hair was curled and piled loosely on her head, with several softly waving locks tumbling down her back, and pink, blue and white sweet peas interwoven throughout, along with a scattering of glistening pearls and sparkling diamond clips.

Diamond and pearl teardrops, which had once belonged to Mattie, dangled from her ears, and a matching necklace with a large, central teardrop diamond hung around her neck.

Her off-the-shoulder, white satin dress with hand stitched pearl, capped sleeves had a tight-fitting bodice, a hand-embroidered waistband of the finest lace, with her name and Jet's sewn in tiny cultured pearls, barely legible unless you stood close, and a delicately flowing full-length skirt with a hand sewn hem of tiny, pale pink, pale blue and white sweet pea flowers, each with a central pearl.

Her veil, also the finest hand-embroidered lace, was interspersed with tiny pearls, a scattering of diamante and edged with the same design as her dress. Even the shoes she wore had white flowers resembling sweet peas stitched on starched and coated lace.

Many photographs were taken of Mia, Lori, Ella and Tiffany before Ella and Tiffany departed to the church in a vintage, white Rolls Royce

Ghost, and Mia and Lori followed behind a few minutes later in another vintage Rolls.

The entrance to St Michael and All Angels was resplendent in white ribbons, pale pink, pale blue, and white floral arrangements, each one containing sweet peas, and the bells rang out, including the melodic Angel Bell as Mia's car approached.

'Are you nervous?' Lori asked as they exited the car.

Mia beamed at her. 'Excited, ecstatic, enthusiastic, but not nervous. I can't wait to be Jet's wife.'

Her veil was arranged to fall softly behind her; she linked her arm through Lori's and as the violins played Johann Pachelbel's Canon in D Major, Mia walked down the aisle towards Jet, with Ella and Tiffany a few steps behind her veil.

The smile on Jet's face made Mia's heart soar, as he stood in the rainbow of light from the stained glass windows bathed in sunshine, his black hair, lustrous and his clean-shaven face even more handsome than it had seemed the day before.

He held a grey top hat and gloves in his hand which he passed to his best man, Justin, as Mia approached. The grey morning suit he wore showed off his frame to perfection, and with his white shirt, a pink, blue and white patterned waistcoat, pale blue cummerbund with matching tie, he took Mia's breath away. And the pink, blue and white sweet peas for his boutonnière, made the ensemble both formal yet casual at the same time.

He didn't take his gaze from Mia and similar to what he had said when he was best man at Hettie and Fred's wedding, he mouthed the words: 'You are beautiful', this time adding: 'I love you, Mia,' when Lori passed Mia's hand to Jet in the formal act of giving her daughter away.

'I love you too,' Mia whispered.

Little M, who was sitting on the floor at the front row on Jet's side of the church, her lead held by Toby, gave a soft bark. Mia and Jet turned to her with loving and reassuring smiles and it seemed as if the dog's mouth curved into a smile too. Her fur gleamed in the sunlight and the circle of sweet peas covering her pink, blue and white patterned collar remained surprisingly intact.

Glen stood before Mia and Jet and smiled; serious as he spoke the formal parts. To Mia's relief, there were no objections as to why the wedding should not proceed. Not that Mia really expected any.

Her friend Anna, one of the women who had helped her overcome her fear of water last summer had said that she might object. She teased Mia on the hen night that there was still a very slight chance she may run down the aisle screaming like a maniac, because she'd always wanted to date Jet Cross. But she had added that she would try to control the urge. It was just a joke, of course, but even so, Mia was glad that part was over.

Mia repeated her vows and said, 'I do,' when asked if she took Jet as her loving husband.

Jet repeated his and when asked if he took Mia, said: 'Absolutely. Yes I do.'

A trumpet of laughter echoed through the church and Jet winked at Mia, his mouth twitching into the grin that she knew and loved so well. It was one of the many things that had made her fall in love with him the very first time she'd seen it.

When told that he could kiss the bride, Jet grinned again, pulling Mia into his arms and kissing her far more passionately than perhaps he should in front of a congregation. Not that Mia was about to protest. In fact she was sorry that it had to end.

They signed the register and a burst of pride shot through Mia. Mia Ward as was. Mia Cross for ever more.

The Flower Duet heralded their exit from the church into the garden at the rear where a host of spring flowers jostled amongst the grass. The Angel Bell rang out until the last photograph was taken but the video continued as the wedding guests followed the bride and groom across a confetti and petal strewn Lane to The Frog and Lily. More ribbons, more flowers and several congratulatory banners and balloons adorned the exterior and interior of the pub.

Outside, in the garden, a huge marquee stood proud, with myriad lights amongst the surrounding hedges and trees, leading down and around posts along the beach, where a large wooden dance floor sat beneath a bright and sunny sky. Later, when the sun set, the sky would turn to pink and purple, violet and orange and the moon and stars would shine upon the throng of happy guests.

Jet was almost close to tears when he saw the silver birch trees, draped with ice-like crystals and hung with messages of good wishes, each one tied with white and silver ribbons.

'You did this for me?' He held Mia tightly in his arms.

'Yes. To show you how much it meant to me when you proposed.'

'This time last year, I saw you for the first time sitting in your car, annoyed that some farmer and his tractor were delaying your journey to Lily Pond Lane. If anyone had told me then, that one year later, you and that farmer would have a wedding on Lily Pond Lane, I would never have believed them.'

'Nor would I. You were rude, annoying, pig-headed and stubborn. And infuriatingly gorgeous, breathtakingly sexy, irritatingly funny with a mesmerising smile. In fact, you're still every single one of those things. Apart from rude, perhaps. Oh and you're very good in bed.'

He laughed and pulled her closer. 'Well, thank you. And you're still incredibly generous, loving and kind. Plus, like me, infuriatingly gorgeous, breathtakingly sexy, irritatingly funny with a mesmerising smile.'

'And?'

'And what? Did I forget something?'

She poked him in the chest with her finger. 'I'm very good in bed.'

'Who told you that?'

'You do. Often.'

'You *are* very good in bed. It's one of the reasons I love you.'

'You loved me before you slept with me.'

'I loved you the moment I saw you. And I'll love you for the rest of my life, Mrs Mia Cross. Now stop talking wife and kiss your husband.'

She smiled. 'I promised to love you but not to obey. But fine. I've got nothing better to do. Not for the next seventy years at least. And just so that you know, I wouldn't want it any other way.'

But there was another surprise, this time for both Mia and Jet. A dinghy waited on the beach to take them to a private yacht anchored a short distance offshore, and fireworks would be let off, shooting into the star-studded blackness of the night sky, from a floating wooden deck tied to the yacht. Something Lori knew her daughter had always dreamt of.

And now that Mia had married Jet, all of Mia's dreams had come true.

'Do you think Mattie's up there looking down on us?' Mia asked, as she danced the evening away with Jet.

'Without a doubt. And smiling because her final mission was a complete and utter success.'

Coming soon

I've loved writing my Lily Pond Lane series and I really hope you've enjoyed each book. I had planned to end this series after Christmas on Lily Pond Lane, but due to the mass of emails and requests on social media for more in this series, I wrote another two, one of which, was this one.

It's now time for me to continue with the other projects I'd put on hold. But the thing is, I love this series as much as you seem to, so it might not be finished yet.

I'll tell you more on my website, in my newsletter and my Facebook, Readers' Club, and also via social media. So please make sure we're connected via at least one of those, to ensure you're in the know.

Other than that, I'll have a new, Christmas book out later this year and I'm also working on a book I've wanted to write for a long time. I'm excited, but it's early days on that one.

A Note from Emily

Thank you for reading this book. A little piece of my heart goes into all of my books and when I send them on their way, I really hope they bring a smile to someone's face. If this book made you smile, or gave you a few pleasant hours of relaxation, I'd love it if you would tell your friends.

I'd be really happy if you have a minute or two to post a review. Just a line will do, and a kind review makes such a difference to my day – to any author's day. Huge thanks to those of you who do so, and for your lovely comments and support on social media. Thank you.

A writer's life can be lonely at times. Sharing a virtual cup of coffee or a glass of wine, or exchanging a few friendly words on Facebook, Twitter or Instagram is so much fun.

You might like to join my Readers' Club by signing up for my newsletter. It's absolutely free, your email address is safe and won't be shared and I won't bombard you, I promise. You can enter competitions and enjoy some giveaways. In addition to that, there's my author page on Facebook and there's also a new Facebook group. You can chat with me and with other fans and get access to my book news, snippets from my daily life, early extracts from my books and lots more besides. Details are on the 'For You' page of my website. You'll find all my contact links in the

Contact section following this.

I'm working on my next book right now. Let's see where my characters take us this time. Hope to chat with you soon.

To see details of my other books, please go to the books page on my website, or scan the QR code below to see all my books on Amazon.

Contact

If you want to be the first to hear Emily's news, find out about book releases, enter competitions and gain automatic entry into her Readers' Club, go to: https://www.emilyharvale.com and subscribe to her newsletter via the 'Sign me up' box. If you love Emily's books and want to chat with her and other fans, ask to join the exclusive Emily Harvale's Readers' Club Facebook group.

Or come and say 'Hello' on Facebook, Twitter and Instagram.

Contact Emily via social media:
www.twitter.com/emilyharvale
www.facebook.com/emilyharvalewriter
www.facebook.com/emilyharvale
www.instagram.com/emilyharvale

Or by email via the website:
www.emilyharvale.com

Printed in Great Britain
by Amazon